D0983817

SILVER
DRAGON CODEX

Books by R.D. Henham

RED DRAGON CODEX

BRONZE DRAGON CODEX

BLACK DRAGON CODEX

BRASS DRAGON CODEX

GREEN DRAGON CODEX

SILVER DRAGON CODEX

GOLD DRAGON CODEX
January 2010

SILVER
DRAGON CODEX

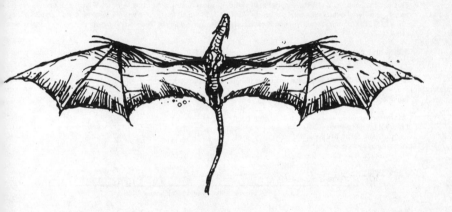

R.D. Henham

MIRRORSTONE

Silver Dragon Codex
©2009 Wizards of the Coast LLC

All characters in this book are fictitious. Any resemblance to actual persons, living or dead, is purely coincidental.

This book is protected under the copyright laws of the United States of America. Any reproduction or unauthorized use of the material or artwork contained herein is prohibited without the express written permission of Wizards of the Coast LLC. The information in this book is based on the lore created for the Dungeons & Dragons® fantasy roleplaying game.

Published by Wizards of the Coast LLC. Mirrorstone, its logo and DUNGEONS & DRAGONS are trademarks of Wizard of the Coast LLC in the U.S.A. and other countries.

All characters, character names, and the distinctive likenesses thereof are property of Wizards of the Coast LLC.

Printed in the U.S.A.

Text by R.D. Henham with assistance from Ree Soesbee
Cover art by Vinod Rams
Interior art by Todd Lockwood
Cartography by Dennis Kauth
First Printing: September 2009

9 8 7 6 5 4 3 2 1

Library of Congress Cataloging-in-Publication Data

Henham, R. D.
 Silver dragon codex / R.D. Henham.
   p. cm.
 "Mirrorstone."
 Summary: A silver dragon who has lost her memory must discover why she attacked and cursed a village.
 ISBN 978-0-7869-5253-3
 [1. Dragons--Fiction. 2. Blessing and cursing--Fiction. 3. Amnesia--Fiction. 4. Circus--Fiction. 5. Fantasy.] I. Title.
 PZ7.H3884Sil 2009
 [Fic]--dc22

                                                                      2009007818

ISBN: 978-0-7869-5253-3
620-24224000-001-EN

U.S., CANADA,   EUROPEAN HEADQUARTERS
ASIA, PACIFIC, & LATIN AMERICA   Hasbro UK Ltd
Wizards of the Coast LLC   Caswell Way
P.O. Box 707   Newport, Gwent NP9 0YH
Renton, WA 98057-0707   GREAT BRITAIN
+1-800-324-6496   Save this address for your records.

Visit our Web site at www.mirrorstonebooks.com

QW - FF   09 10 11 12 13 14 15

DEDICATED TO ALL THOSE WHO HAVE EVER HAD TO JUGGLE EIGHT THINGS AT ONCE. COUNT YOURSELVES LUCKY THAT THEY WEREN'T BLADED, SPINNING, AND ON FIRE.

—R.D.H.

FOR THE REAL BELEN, WHO SPENDS A GREAT DEAL OF HER TIME IN THE SPOTLIGHT, BUT STILL MANAGES TO LOVE HER AUDIENCE AS MUCH AS THEY LOVE HER.

—R.S.

Dear Honored Scribe Henham,

I must confess, were I not wizardly inclined I think I might like to be in a circus. I could put on silly costumes to make everyone laugh, or I could do magic tricks to make them gasp, or ride atop giant beasts, or do acrobatics while hanging from ropes dangling from high rafters!

Granted, I've done about all of that on my many and varied adventures, but never with an audience to cheer me on. What could be more fun?

It was with great excitement, then, that I got to investigate this latest dragon tale, as it began and ended in a fantastic traveling circus. As mentioned in my last letter, even your hard-working messenger enjoyed the show!

But not everything in this particular circus was as it seemed. From little things such as invisible servants who cleaned the grounds, to not so little things such as a human performer with a secret past she can't remember, something definitely wasn't quite right under the big top!

I've enclosed my notes and sketches of this high-flying and thrilling tale. In it you'll read all about a girl named Belen and her desperate quest to clear her name after an accusation that she is a destructive silver dragon—all while discovering the secrets of the circus in which she's been performing ever since waking up with no memories of who she used to be.

I hope you enjoy this tale of intrigue and excitement as much as I did! I will have another tale for you before too long, so make sure to send your messenger back soon—I'm heading to the north where I've heard rumors of adventures involving a magnificent gold dragon that will surely spark your imagination.

All my best,

Sindri Suncatcher

Celebrated Commentator on Circuses and the (Potential) Dragons Therein

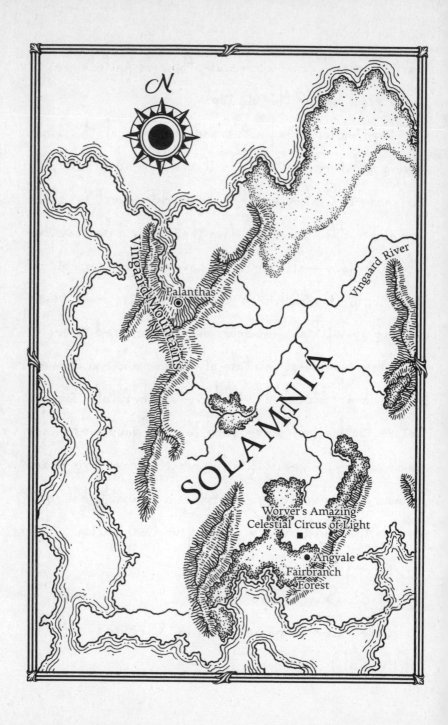

PROLOGUE

Belen sighed, staring up at the trapeze. Her silvery hair reflected a trickle of the spotlight, which glinted past the heavy, red velvet curtains. She shifted her feet in their ballet slippers, flexing her toes. She closed her eyes and listened to the applause, the shouts of eager children, the roar of a happy crowd—the sounds of home.

Opening her eyes, she reached for her tremendous fans, pulling the stiff metal handles through her fingers. Every performance was a rush and every burst of cheered applause lifted her heart, making her feel almost as if she, too, could fly like the trapeze artists now so far above the ring. But even amid all that happiness . . . something was missing. She never spoke of it, never told anyone—that would seem ungrateful. Belen was thankful for all that the little circus had done for her. They'd found her and given her purpose when she was lost and alone.

She loved to dance, to feel the graceful movements, the powerful spins and swift turns, the leaps that felt almost like taking flight. If anything, the performances always ended too soon, leaving her standing in a melting puddle of spotlight to come to her senses, once more alone on the ground.

Was it the end of the dance that made her sad?

Belen shook her head, trying to rid herself of the doubt. Preshow jitters, nothing more, she told herself. There was nothing to be afraid of, no reason to be sad. She'd performed this dance a thousand times and knew every twirl and lunge by heart. Still, she knew what was coming when the music ended. Why did she always feel sad when she was finished dancing?

Jace passed by her, touched her elbow, and wished her luck in a faint whisper as the music in the ring swelled to a crescendo. The act on stage was almost finished. Belen smiled at him and looked around at the many friends who surrounded her. She knew them all by name, knew their habits and their laughter. They were almost like family.

Something in her heart twinged, and Belen shuddered from the top of her head to the tip of her toes. She managed to brush away a tear without smearing her greasepaint.

Belen lifted the feathered dancing fans, painted on her smile, and stepped out onto the stage.

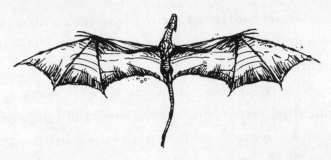

CHAPTER ONE

"Ladies and gentlemen! Children of all ages!" a booming voice rumbled out, echoing with the strange tinniness of magical enhancement. "I welcome you to the one, the only, the grandest stage of all—Worver's Amazing Celestial Circus of Light!"

Lights came up, blazing over the crowd. The silk panels of the tent fluttered in the breeze of a thousand hands clapping and feet stomping, the crowd cheering at the grand pageant put on before them. Dancing dogs cavorted around the outside of the ring, jumping through hoops to entertain children. Trapeze artists in shining tights waved from the ceiling, swaying back and forth over a wide net.

Jace stood behind the curtain at the rear of the show, peeping out between the folds as he prepared for his turn on stage. He had to look past the cage that held the arcox—a horrible lobster-clawed creature with chitinous armor and scuttling, clawlike legs beneath its shell—to try and make out the act occurring in the farthest ring. He certainly wasn't going to get any closer, not with that cage parked there!

Act after act regaled the crowd with wonders, all organized into perfect harmony by the red-coated ringmaster, Worver. A massive minotaur named Hautos lifted wagons over his head, stacking them one by one. As a finale, he lifted three at once. Ebano Saham, the Mysterious Mystic, narrowed his strange purple eyes as he used the power of his mind to convince audience members that they were chickens.

After a pair of lions stalked from the ring, the ringmaster's hand flew up as if to catch the spotlight. The red tails of his coat fluttered about, and he doffed his top hat grandly as he bowed with a flourish. His thick, black mustache curled up at the ends. His pristine cuffs and collar wavered stiffly under a heavily starched coat. At his side, an agile creature the size of a small monkey danced and cavorted, wearing a clown's white ruffle around its neck. The strange little pet was covered in grayish fur, glitter painted on the horns that twisted from its head. Wherever the ringmaster went, his funny pet went with him, dancing at his heels and begging for treats sprinkled from his pockets. Worver gestured and the creature danced, bouncing on its rear legs and waving its head back and forth so that the horns on its head glinted in the bright light. Charmed, the audience roared in approval.

There was only one performance before Jace's finale. The headliner of the circus was about to go on. Jace never missed her performance. He'd seen her dance every night since she joined the circus almost five years ago.

"Our next enticement." Worver swept a white-gloved hand toward the ceiling. Chattering shrilly, his pet leaped up onto his shoulder. "Ladies and gentlemen, may I present to you the finest dancer on Krynn! She's performed for crowned heads of state, major wizards, noble knights. She's danced from ocean to ocean! The one, the only . . . the incomparable Lady Belen!"

The spotlight expanded on a beautiful young woman at the center of the main ring. In her early twenties, luminous with the flush of youth, she stood poised and delicate as the ringmaster introduced her. Her skin was porcelain, long hair the color of starlight on a spiderweb. Her gray eyes opened wide to greet the audience as she bowed regally before them, and in each hand, she held a wide silver folding fan as long as she was tall.

Jace caught himself sighing and glanced around quickly to make sure no one had noticed. Belen was older than he by a handful of years, and she was the most beautiful woman he'd ever seen.

"Born in a mystic land to royalty that reigned long before the Cataclysm but has since been lost, the Lady Belen is the last of a truly noble line . . ." Ringmaster Worver continued with the introduction, expounding on the strange magical event that brought the Lady Belen to dance at the Amazing Celestial Circus of Light. The audience ate it up as Worver shaped outrageous images with his words—an ancient land, a forlorn queen, her only daughter cast into loneliness, a thousand years out of time . . .

Her head humbly bowed for the introduction, Belen glanced back under thick lashes and caught Jace's eye. With an impish wink, she smiled at him. Jace's heart sped up and he tugged the curtain tighter, hoping no one in the audience could see him.

"Almost ready?" The hiss in Jace's ear made him jump. One of the jugglers—Cerisse—thumped his back. Cerisse was his age, born and raised in the circus just as he had been. She giggled and looked through the curtains out to the ring. "Oh, I see what's going on . . . it's Belen's turn to perform. Were you staring at her again?" Cerisse's tone was teasing, but as sharp as the daggers she juggled onstage.

There was no way to hide the fact that he'd been watching, so Jace grinned sheepishly and ran a hand through his dark blond hair. "She's amazing."

"Yeah." Cerisse's smile faded and she looked past him onto the stage. "She is." Together, they pulled the curtain back and peeked together.

"Do you think the story Worver's peddling is true? That she's a princess?"

"Not a chance." Cerisse snorted. "She's probably the daughter of a goat washer from Northern Ergoth. He changes it every time he introduces her, and every time she smiles as if it's true. Belen's been here five years, and still has never told anyone where she comes from or why she's here." Cerisse shrugged, the long braid of her auburn hair swinging back and forth behind her shoulders. "If she doesn't care, why should we? Belen brings in crowds, and we all make money. That's all that matters."

Jace couldn't tear his eyes off Belen, even to respond to Cerisse. The silver-haired woman stood alone in the center of the ring. More graceful than wind on water, Belen lifted her arms, snapping the two metal fans into perfect half-circle arcs. The steel ribs of the fans jutted out just a few inches above their metallic arc—a fact that became clearly noticeable when the end of each rib burst into flame. The audience oohed and aahed, and she turned the props in her hands to show the movement, her hair blowing in the wind the fans generated when they moved. Belen spun the two blazing fans, leaving ethereal trails in the air where the

7

fans passed. Soft music played, slow and lilting, and she began to dance.

Jace watched her, smiling. It was clear why she'd so quickly gained prominence in the circus, rising from an assistant to a headlining act over the last five years. He'd worked circuses since he was a child, and he'd never seen anyone with her grace and beauty. Jace sighed, as entranced as the rest of her audience.

"Jace, you idiot, wake up!" Cerisse smacked him harder. "You should be getting ready!"

He blinked. "How much longer do I have?"

"Belen's act lasts six minutes. When she finishes, you need to be ready to scale to the high platform." Cerisse pointed, smile tight beneath her white greasepaint. "Are you sure you want to do this?"

The tightrope stretched—almost invisible—a hundred feet in the air. Jace stared, frowning. Just a rope. Just a thread of hemp between two poles. Jace had walked it a thousand times, trained on it since he was a child. His father had too, and his grandfather. Jace came from a long line of circus folk. There was nothing to be afraid of, he told himself. Accidents . . . were rare.

"I'll be ready," Jace said, but his voice cracked.

"You'd better be," Cerisse said, patting his shoulder. "They aren't putting up a net."

"Yeah. I told them not to. That's how it has to be done." A sinking feeling chilled Jace's bones. He closed his eyes, trying to imagine the feel of the rope beneath his feet. Nothing to worry about, he told himself. I've done this in practice a hundred times.

Then again, so had Dad.

Jace shook himself, trying to settle his nerves. He could do it. There was no difference between doing it on stage and in practice. The audience signaled Belen's finale with an awed rush of applause that pounded through the seats.

"All right, here she comes. She's taking her last bow." Cerisse pulled back the curtain and gestured. "The lights go out . . . right about now!"

Beyond the curtain, Worver waved his top hat as Belen waved once more to the crowd. The brilliant lights spangled from her silver dress, fans glittering in delicate hands as she saluted the stomping, cheering crowd. When the light faded, Jace could hear the soft padding of her feet as she turned and ran toward them. Without so much as rippling the soft fabric, Belen swept through the parted velvet and sat down on a nearby crate.

"Oh, Jace! Cerisse! Were you watching?" Jace felt a warm glow settle in his stomach as Belen looked at him, setting her fans down. Her neck and shoulders were daubed in sweat from the dance, her breath coming in puffs. A moment after her fans were set down, an invisible stagehand lifted them. Soft cloths began scrubbing the metal grooves, held by invisible hands. Belen hardly noticed, murmuring a polite thanks to the invisible helpers before turning to Jace. "Was it a good performance?" Belen's delicate features were pressed with worry. "I think I messed up one of the steps . . ."

"You looked great. Even if you did, I didn't notice a thing, so the audience definitely couldn't tell." Jace beamed as brightly as the fire that had lit the fans. "Wonderful, as usual. Perfect." He couldn't stop talking. "You were amazing."

When Belen wasn't looking, Cerisse rolled her eyes.

"You're such a good friend to say that." Belen shook out her silver hair. "I was so nervous. I had a strange feeling that something was going to go wrong tonight, something terrible. But nothing happened, did it?" She shrugged and turned a little red. "I guess it was just silliness."

Jace started to answer, but choked on the words as Cerisse started shoving him toward the climbing pole. "I have to go . . ."

"Oh!" Belen blinked. "That's right! You're the finale! No time to chatter on, then. We'll talk later. Fortune find you, Jace. I'll be watching!" Belen pressed his hand between hers, leaving a bit of glitter on his palm before she stepped away.

She'd be watching? Jace gulped again. With no time to spare, he ran forward into the darkness.

When he reached the edge of the main ring, Jace grasped the handholds on the pole holding the wire aloft. Puffs of chalk rose where he set his hands. All around him, the darkened ring was a flurry of activity though he stood there alone. Ropes above jerked, seeming to tie themselves to stiff poles that held the structure aloft, and rakes floated out from the rear to scratch the ground flat beneath the wire. An unseen hand swept up popcorn from the edges of the ring, and another tightened the pins that held the pole in the ground. Two workers oversaw the net's removal, and Jace stared with a bit of longing as it was carefully untied, dropped to the ground, and then rolled neatly away. She'd be watching.

His heart fluttered, and it wasn't just from the height.

Jace climbed hand over hand up the pole, pulling himself higher and higher above the ground. The rainbow-striped canvas of the big-top roof stretched like a wide sky above him. The faces of men, women, and children flowed like a sea below. And the only thing between him and the hard-packed dirt was a single thin rope, just more than forty feet long. Signaling with a broad gesture, Jace let Ringmaster Worver know he was ready. Now or never.

"Aaaaaand now," Worver's voice boomed out, "our finale! Ladies and gentlemen, listen to my story carefully—tonight is a very special night!" He lowered the tone of his voice to a conspiratorial murmur, the sound still carrying clearly through the tent via some sort of magical amplification. Eager for more, the audience riveted its attention on him, a living thing focused on Worver's every move.

"Five years ago in this very tent, a brilliant star flamed—and was extinguished. Jordan Pettier, Jordan the Undaunted, attempted the first and only netless quadruple tuck flip to ever be performed in any circus anywhere on Krynn! He made that attempt on the very high wire you now see strung above you. I say 'attempt,' ladies and gentlemen, because to this day that trick has never been successfully performed.

"Jordan the Undaunted gave it his very best . . . and failed."

The spotlight focused first on the wire, and then on Jace, blinding him with its brilliance. He struggled to smile though he couldn't see anything, and tried to think of anything but the huge, gaping chasm ahead of him.

"Jordan never set foot on that tightrope again, and it has never been strung in the big top, in honor of his memory.

His passing was as if a candle had been snuffed—the best and brightest among us, extinguished in his prime. A tragedy, my good people, of the highest sort. But tonight, ladies and gentlemen, Worver's Amazing Celestial Circus of Light will right that wrong and change history forever!" A wave of applause shook the tent, rippling from silk-seamed wall to hard-packed floor.

"Above you, the untested, untried—but ready to face his father's memory—Jace Pettier, son of Jordan the Undaunted!" Jace gulped as he was introduced, trying to keep the smile plastered on his face. Worver's words were a bit of an exaggeration. True, he'd never performed this trick before, but a lifetime of learning how to be a circus acrobat made him anything but untested.

Worver raised both hands, his implike pet dancing around his knees. "Tonight, Jace will perform for you the same trick that felled his father. Before this audience, he will redeem the name of Pettier and prove that they are, once more, the finest high-wire family ever to perform on Krynn!

"On behalf of the entire Amazing Celestial Circus of Light, I ask that you remember any slip of the foot or loss of concentration could cause the same catastrophe! May we have silence for the brave young man, if you please!"

Drums softly rolled beneath the oohing of the crowd as Jace stepped out onto the high wire. His steps firm and certain, he walked along it far above the dirt floor of the ring, waving his arms to either side in greeting to the wide-eyed spectators below. First, he did a few passes on the rope to show the audience his skill. The rope was strong beneath his feet. He turned around, clearing a single jump into the air to test the high wire's stiffness. With more surety, Jace allowed the rebound of the wire's bounce to snap him up again, twisting his body into a single flip before he landed squarely back on the thick rope. The crowd burst into short-lived applause, once more quieted by the ringmaster's carefully timed call for silence.

"Are you ready, young Jace?" Worver swept his hat from his head and placed it over his heart, looking up at him with an exaggerated tremble. "Are you certain? You could turn back now, my boy, before all is lost . . ." Good old Worver, playing it up right to the end. The audience stared, its focus a palpable thing, like a weight on Jace's shoulders. As planned, he waved twice in acknowledgement, and the drumroll swept to a crescendo. Worver stepped back, out of the spotlight, and Jace spread his arms to either side.

He would need a great deal of snap from the rope to throw him high enough to complete four whole rolls in the air before he landed again. Three was the most that any other circus performer had done, even with a net. Four was considered impossible—but he'd done it in practice, and his father had done it before a crowd . . . well, until his foot slipped on the landing and he fell the long distance to the ring below. No. Jace shook his head. *I can't think about that right now.*

Never look at the ground. He heard his father's voice remind him from their lessons when Jace was still a child. *Never look down. Not even when you're falling. It doesn't help.*

Jace decided that he'd jump on three. One. The rope wove up and down with the pressure of his legs. Two. Jace leaned into the bounce, aware that he would need every bit of thrust to make the revolutions. He had to have enough power to flip him four times in the air, but not so much that he didn't land squarely on the rope once that last somersault was completed. Jace was ready. He'd practiced even more than his father, and he was lighter, younger, more agile. This was going to work, and he was going to be famous. More, his father's name—the Pettier name—would once again be redeemed, and his father's legacy would be secured!

Thr—

"Hold!" The voice cracked through the air like a whip. Jace's foot slipped in shock, jolted up by the rope despite his sudden attempt to freeze. His concentration ruined, Jace felt everything tilt around him. The rope snapped beneath the balls of his feet, pitching sideways, cracking against his ankle as his leg twisted to the side. The world reeled, faces in the crowd blurring into a haze. Jace hurled one hand out to try and catch the wire as he fell past it, but the rough rope brushed against his fingertips.

Stupid! I was stupid to try. The thoughts exploded in his head with the sickening reel of sudden one-way flight. The image of his father lying on the floor beneath the rope, gasping for breath, his back broken, flashed into Jace's mind. I wanted to make Dad proud, to redeem our name, to wipe away the fear . . . I was an idiot . . . an idiot . . .

A horrible, painful jerk shook Jace's frame, and suddenly his fall slowed. He hovered above the ground, breeze rippling his hair as he floated softly back and forth like a feather. Jace squirmed around in the strange grip of magic as the ground swept nearer, drifting up to meet him. While upside down, he stared at the people in the highest bleachers, eye to eye with their screaming children. The crowd was on its feet—not quite for the reason he'd planned on getting them there—staring in shock and horror. Worver was standing in the aisle, frozen in amazement. Everyone gawked as a man in flowing white robes stepped over the wooden edge of the ring.

"Hold," the man in white robes said again. "I am here to arrest that woman." His finger jabbed out, focusing on Belen. She gasped, and two of the clowns nearby stepped forward as though to protect the delicate dancer. Jace watched it all as he slowly sailed down under the wizard's power. "You should never have returned to Solamnia, Belen."

"Arrest her? On what charge? Who are you?" Ringmaster Worver puffed up, settling his hat low against his brow. He stepped toward Belen, placing an arm around the dancer's slim shoulders.

"My name is Mysos, of the White Robes of Palanthas. The charge is murder." The wizard settled his arms over his chest and Jace hit the ground with an echoing thud.

ace wrung his chalked hands. Everything had gone wrong—his trick, now this. What was that White Robe doing, and who did he think he was? Jace glared at Mysos as the wizard walked among them, but Jace said nothing. Mysos's dark eyes were as hard as flint chips. His robes had seemed white and clean under the spotlight, but now Jace could see that they were stained by travel.

Worver made the clowns escort the audience off the circus grounds—the people didn't get their money back, of course, but everyone was given paper pinwheels for the children in order to apologize for cutting the show short. The expense was minimal, but the embarrassment was tremendous, and stress showed in every etched line of the ringmaster's face. He shooed performers from his wagon with wide swipes of his top hat, thumping more than one when they moved too slowly out of the way. "Nothing to see here," he snarled at them. "Get back to your tents and

18

wagons. We've got another show tomorrow morning, and I'll dock the pay of anyone who comes in late or unrehearsed!" His threats were enough to scatter most of them, but some, such as the enigmatic mesmerist with the strange eyes, were less impressed. Ebano simply pulled his silky purple robes tight about his shoulders and glared down the bridge of his dark nose at the shorter ringmaster.

Worver sighed at Ebano, pushing past with a mutter. "Useless old fool, can't even speak a proper language. Hautos!" Worver called to the minotaur strongman. "Keep everyone away from the door."

"Jace, come with me. I don't want to go alone." Belen didn't let go of his arm, her eyes wide and frightened. Worver nodded subtly, eyes glancing from the boy to the wizard as if gauging how much Mysos would let the circus folk do.

Jace gulped, but nodded. He tried to straighten up and puff out his chest—he wouldn't let anything hurt Belen—but under Ebano's hawklike eyes, he deflated. What was an acrobat going to do against a White Robe of Palanthas? Do cartwheels for him? Also, he couldn't stop looking at Belen. A murderer? Really? The idea was outrageous. Hautos stepped in front of the crowd, crossing his thick arms over his bull-like chest. The brass ring in his pierced nose twitched with eagerness. He clearly wanted to fight someone, and from what Jace knew of him, Hautos didn't particularly care if it was Mysos or Ebano. The glaring minotaur didn't like anyone who used magic—and he did his best to make sure everyone knew it.

Leaving Hautos and Ebano outside the wagon, Jace, Belen, Mysos and the ringmaster clambored inside, closing the door behind them.

Once inside, Worver's carefully constructed façade fell instantly. He started fuming, steam practically rising out from under his head. Mysos, on the other hand, was coolly confident, keeping Belen always in his sight like a hawk that had spotted a rabbit. Jace stood awkwardly, mostly because Belen refused to let go of his arm. The glitter on her cheeks was smudged. "Don't worry," Jace whispered. "I'm sure this is all a misunderstanding."

"Preposterous," Worver was already saying before Mysos even had a chance to repeat the charges. "Belen hasn't killed anyone." Glowing eyes floated in the dusky light as the ringmaster's strange pet followed him to the back of the wagon. It chattered and leaped from the floor to the desk to his shoulder, its tail twisting around its master's arm as the odd, slick-furred beast scolded them all. "There there, Tsusu," Worver soothed his pet. "We'll get to the bottom of this, never you fear." The creature chirruped and rubbed its head against his hand.

"Do you know this woman so well," the White Robe

rumbled, "that you would risk your circus, your livelihood, and the well-being of all those who work here—on her word?" When the ringmaster quailed, Mysos allowed himself a thin smile. "Let me tell you a story, ringmaster, about a small town of Solamnia not far from here. Angvale is only a few hours to the south, within the wood of Fairbranch. A quiet village. A peaceful folk."

"Sounds like a nice place," Jace muttered.

Mysos had good ears. He turned to face the young high-wire walker. "It was, until it was destroyed by a dragon." Jace stopped dead in his mental tracks. Dragon? As in the War of the Lance? As in, fire in the sky and cities burning? That kind of dragon?

Worver's top hat slipped between his fingers, thumping to the floor. His pet squeaked in surprise, dodging, then climbed up onto Worver's shoulder. The ringmaster stammered, "Wait, wait. A dragon? There's no dragon here! You said Belen—"

"Belen is a dragon. *The* dragon, in fact, that destroyed Angvale," Mysos said.

Worver choked. Belen whitened. Jace thought he heard a snort of surprise from outside the door. Jace could hear Hautos shuffling just outside the door, his heavy hooves scraping on the wooden stairs. In a few breaths, everyone in the circus would know. The

White Robe continued. "The dragon attacked without provocation and without warning. She was relentless. She was brutal. None within the village survived. The tale was told only by those who lived far outside the village and saw the dragon flying overhead." Mysos stared at the quaking Belen and said, "Once the dragon murdered everyone in the village, she took human form in order to hide from her crimes, and fled Solamnia. But I set a spell that would tell me if that dragon ever set foot here again—and now she has. I have followed the trace of that spell here. It leads"—he stared down at her—"to you."

Mysos turned his head, allowing Belen to escape his cold stare, and fixed his eyes on the ringmaster. "You will deliver Belen to me, Master Worver, or I will take her by force."

"I didn't do it!" Belen gasped. "I haven't killed anyone!"

"But you admit you are that dragon?" Mysos was stern.

"I'm not a dragon!" Belen said, her muscles clenched. "At least, I don't think . . . I don't remember . . ." She fell silent, her gaze falling to the floor.

Wringing his hands, Worver moaned, "It can't be true. You must understand, Belen is very well loved here. Why, I've practically taken the girl in as my daughter. She's never shown any sign of ill temper or vice. We found Belen wandering in the woods to the south of here, during the circus's last pass through this area—nearly five years ago, I believe it was. The poor young girl was confused—she had no memory of her past, her name, or what she was doing there. We took her in—"

"Very kind of you," Mysos murmured satirically.

" . . . Offered her a warm bed, a safe haven. In return, she worked for the circus. First she performed odd jobs, but it became quickly clear that she had a great talent. Thanks to her, and the rest of my fine performers, our circus has gone from obscurity to . . . to . . . renowned!" Worver tugged at his coat nervously. "I don't know if you saw her perform, my lord wizard, but Belen is an exceptional dancer, one of the best I've ever seen. She's made the circus a great deal of money. She's been sweet, gentle . . . honest . . ." Worver fumbled for words.

Mysos was impatient. "And you never once asked where she came from?"

Stiffening, Worver snapped, "We're a circus, not a magistrate. A lot of people here have questionable pasts. More than a few of them are running from something. I don't ask questions."

"Then I'm sure you won't mind if I do." Mysos turned away from the ringmaster, evoking another hiss from Tsusu.

The White Robe addressed Belen sharply. "Belen, do you deny that you are a dragon?"

"Don't ask me—I don't remember!" Belen answered. "The ringmaster is correct. I have no memory beyond when I first saw the circus. My first memory is of seeing circus tents through the trees and making my way toward them. I was wandering in the forest, wearing nothing but rags. I was hurt—my legs and arms were cut, torn by forest brush, we think. I know that I was upset, but I don't remember why. There's nothing before that." Belen was standing firmly on widespread feet, but her legs were shaking and her hand still gripped Jace's arm. She opened her mouth again to say more, but her voice failed, and she fell quiet, eyes blazing.

Jace couldn't stand to see his friend so shaken. "Sir wizard," he addressed the mage. "What proof do you have that Belen is responsible?" Mysos seemed to realize that Jace was in the room for the first time, taking in the boy's brightly colored tights and wind-rumpled hair with a quick assessment. "She's my friend, and she's always been kind—to me, and to the people of the circus. We can't just let her go with you unless we're sure you speak the truth."

When the wizard spoke, his voice was somewhat kinder. "You're the tightrope walker, Jace Pettier, aren't you?" Jace nodded, surprised that the wizard knew his name. "I was a fan of your father's when I was a child. His death was a very great tragedy, son. You have my sympathies." Jace blinked at the unexpected kindness, surprised to see a bit of humanity beneath the White Robe's stony demeanor.

"My spell used these to track the dragon." Mysos reached into a pouch at his side, drawing forth three shining objects that Jace thought at first were silver coins. Mysos placed them in Jace's hands. They were lighter than money—thin and supple, with the texture and resilience of leather, not metal. "These are dragon scales. They were collected at the village, and they belonged to the silver dragon that attacked Angvale. I took them from the ruins of the buildings that were destroyed, where the dragon had scraped herself on the rubble. On that day, five years ago, I cast a spell on these scales to help me find the dragon, but she had passed beyond the scope of my magic. A few days ago, the tracking spell began to work again. Watch."

The wizard moved one hand through the air above the scales, and a soft white light emanated from them. A pale, greenish smoke rose from the three silver crescents, hovering in the air before drifting directly toward Belen. Jace stepped back and forth, holding the scales in his palm. No matter where he moved them, the smoke continued to drift toward the young woman. "They began to smoke when she re-entered Solamnia," Mysos explained. "I simply followed the direction of the magical compass until I arrived here. While she was performing, I walked around the edge of the stage. I'm quite certain the trail leads toward your friend."

Belen made a soft noise, her attention focused on the scales. "But if I was really a dragon," she whispered, "wouldn't I remember?"

"Shock, most likely." Mysos's voice was hard again, but not as angry as it had sounded before. "These scales are silver, as was the dragon that shed them. Such dragons, metallic dragons, are creatures of good. For one to perform such a horrible act of vengeance and cruelty is entirely against their character. Nevertheless, this dragon performed a horrible, villainous act. Villagers on the outskirts of town saw the silver dragon sweep through the trees, attack buildings with its claws, and rip the village apart. Only a few escaped with their lives. The rest . . . were lost.

"I myself saw the cold, snowy traces of a silver dragon's breath in the wreckage, and the unmistakable marks of dragon claws in the ground. If any other dragon had been in the area that day, those fleeing villagers would have seen it—there would have been some other mark." Mysos spoke matter-of-factly, arms folded. "There was only one dragon, and the village was destroyed."

"All . . . dead?" Belen whispered, her face paling. "Everyone in the village?"

"Destroyed or eaten by the dragon," Mysos answered. "Only a few who were far away, out in the forest, escaped. They said they saw a silver dragon swooping down over the trees toward the village."

"That's no proof at all!" Jace blurted out. "They didn't actually see the dragon do anything. Even if it was Belen, she could have been there to fight some other evil. Belen, do you remember anything about this village? Anything at all?"

"I'm trying," she said, squeezing his hand. "There's nothing but darkness. I can't remember." She looked up at him, tears in the corners of her eyes. "I can't imagine destroying an entire village, killing all those people, even if I had the power to do so. It just doesn't feel right. I wouldn't hurt anyone, Jace. If it was me, I must have had a reason. I must have been tricked, or under the power of some evil magic."

On Worver's shoulder, the slick-furred gray animal crooned. "There, there, dear," Worver said, patting Belen's hand. "I believe you. These charges sound completely ridiculous." Belen grasped Worver's hand, and the pudgy man smiled beneath his thick handlebar mustache. "We're not going to let you go without a fight, my dear girl, I can grant you that." The ringmaster's words were brave, but his eyes flicked to Mysos as if he expected the White Robe to take out a ruler and smack him across the back of his hand for such impudence.

Jace stepped forward. "Master Mysos? Since Belen's been here, she's been good to everyone. She helps with chores, goes out of her way to watch the children when other people are rehearsing, and she's never so much as hurt a fly. You can't arrest her when she doesn't remember anything."

"Oh, can't I?" Mysos raised a thick eyebrow. "And why not?"

"Because it wouldn't be fair!" Jace argued. "You can't have a trial if she can't remember anything. Belen gets a chance to argue on her own behalf, right? If she can't justify what happened or find witnesses to prove her story, then it's just a sham. You said silver dragons don't do this kind of thing. If someone forced her into it, or faked her attack, then *they're* the real criminal."

Mysos pondered this. "Well, the circumstances are highly unusual. But still, I have proof these scales found at the ruined site belong to her. I have witnesses that place her at the village of Angvale on the day it was destroyed, and I have clear signs of a dragon attack on that village. That is enough proof for most judges to convict."

"Not if she can't argue her side," Jace said quietly. "You said you respected my father. Then you must have known that he had a reputation as an honorable man. I ask you to trust my word as you would have trusted his. Give us a little time to help Belen remember what happened. We won't run away or hide, but let us look for the truth." Jace met Mysos's eyes squarely. He tried not to bite his lip, hoping the White Robe's dubious look would fade. "The circus isn't supposed to leave this area for three days. Give me three days to help her remember."

"And if I do?" The wizard raised a bushy eyebrow.

"Then I promise that I'll go with you—willingly," Belen offered. "If I really did what you claim and hurt all those people, then I *should* be judged for it. You won't have any trouble with me."

"No, Belen, really, I must insist." Worver stood up, starting at the idea. "This man means to lock you away—or worse! I can't allow it, no matter what the cost, my dear. You can't leave the circus. It's your home—we're your family." The ringmaster paced in front of them, clearly upset.

"Master Worver, it's the only way." Belen looked up at him. "You've been like a father to me for five years, but you can't protect me from my past. Someone has to find out what happened. I'm going to go into those woods where I was found, seek out the village, and discover the truth."

"My goodness, no! Let me ask Hautos to look into it. Find a priest to cast an augury." The ringmaster floundered, mustache drooping. "You shouldn't risk yourself. It's very dangerous out there in those woods!"

"It has to be me," Belen said in a very small voice. "It's my history. If I am a dragon . . . well, who knows? Remembering that can't be all bad, can it? And if I can help right this wrong, then it's worth risking whatever danger is out there. Don't worry, ringmaster. You've been so good to me, giving me a home here in the circus, helping me when I was hurt and lost. I won't forget that, but I can't ignore this either, nor let someone else look into it for me. This is something I have to do for myself."

Worver sank down into an armchair with a groan. His little pet, Tsusu, snatched up a circus program and began to fan him with the edge, making the ringmaster's curled black mustache quaver. "My poor girl. My poor circus! I'm going to faint. I think I'm going to just drop dead right here in the wagon. Water, please?" Jace quickly poured a glass from a pitcher nearby, and Worver drank it down with a choking sort of gulp. Belen pressed the ringmaster's hand between hers.

The White Robe watched all of this in surprise. "Well, I must admit, I'm not used to trusting criminals, or letting them go—even temporarily—once I've found them. Still, this situation is highly unusual, and silver dragons have never been known to be violent toward innocents."

He stared down at the woman in silver glitter, his fingers tapping against the sleeve of his robe. He wrinkled his lip and tilted his head in internal debate.

"Very well," the wizard said at last. "I will remain here with the circus. Should you flee, abandon your purpose, or in any case not turn yourself in on the third day from today, the circus will pay a hefty penalty. I can assure you, the cost will be so many pieces of steel that it will put this circus completely out of business."

There was a small moan from Worver, who dropped the empty water glass.

"All the performers—the animals—the tents! We'd have to sell everything, let everyone go," the ringmaster gasped. "We'd be ruined!"

"Don't worry, Master Worver," Jace said, his heart leaping even as Ringmaster Worver shrank further into the chair. "We won't let you down."

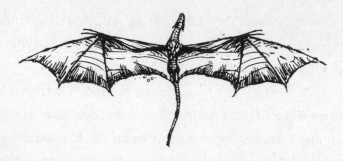

Chapter Three

"Three days?" Cerisse, the juggler, tugged on her long auburn braid as if she might pull herself around in circles. Her face was long and sorrowful, filled with indecision. "Only three days? It will take a day to get to the village and back, so you'll only have two days to snoop around. What if there's nothing there?"

"This one must agree." The purple-robed mesmerist crossed his arms regally. His voice was strange and flowing, the unfamiliar syllables of Jace's language fumbling on Ebano's tongue. The mystic spoke only a little bit of Common, mostly restricted to the pat phrases that Worver had made him memorize for his act. Ebano could go on and on about the "movement of the stars" or the "shrouded future," but when he had to communicate on his own, he was pretty well stumped. He also couldn't figure out the word "I," so most of the time he used his own name or just "this one." Like all the other strange folk in the circus, Jace just took Ebano in stride. The foreigner was an excellent hypnotist, and that's what kept the crowds coming in—not his conversational skills. "This one thinks . . . how you say? . . . danger." Ebano's voice changed, took on the deeper timbre of stagecraft as he intoned one of his rote lines. "I see dark clouds in your future."

Jace rolled his eyes. "Yes, Ebano, I know. Dark clouds. You've said that three times." Jace continued stuffing bread rolls and a bit of sausage into his travel sack and checked his water skin to be sure it was full. Belen had gone back to her tent to change clothes and pack. Jace shared his wagon with Cerisse and Ebano. They'd followed him back and refused to leave, wringing the story out of him drop by drop. Forced to talk while he packed or lose valuable time, Jace ducked around them while he struggled to remember anything he'd need in the woods. "We have to go. If we don't, Belen is put on trial without any evidence to prove her innocence."

"Jace, I'm just saying, how do you know you'll find anything?" Cerisse ventured, shifting from foot to foot. When Jace glared at her, she stomped one foot and waved her hands to ward him off. "I'm not saying Belen's guilty! I'm just saying that it's been five years. What if there's no evidence left to find? You shouldn't risk yourself—"

"Belen's going," he growled, "so I'm going. We'll find something."

Ebano lifted his hand and passed it through the air, pausing to show them a card that had suddenly appeared between his fingers. "Ah." He muttered rapidly in his strange, chirping tongue. Working to find the words, the tall, thin man fumbled for the lines he used on stage and came up with, "Much danger in your future. Dark clouds."

"Ebano, I know. I know how to fight—a little—and for the most part we should be safe. There's nothing out there, remember? Mysos said the village was abandoned."

"But what if . . . I mean . . . she's . . . the village . . ." Cerisse shook her head, her braid swinging about like a striking serpent. "What if she remembers and it's not good? The dragon that attacked the village ate the people in it!"

"You think Belen would hurt me? Hurt any of us?" Jace snatched one of his clean shirts and stuffed it in the knapsack. "Not a chance."

"Ah." Ebano hummed, brightening. "I have it. Not go alone. This one goes also." He dropped his voice and intoned dramatically, "The gods have decided."

"What?" Jace nearly dropped the bag. "You can't—"

"That's a good idea, Ebano!" Cerisse brightened. "I'm going too!"

"You . . . hey!"

"Don't be jealous, Jace," Cerisse sniffed. "Belen is our friend as well as yours. She watches my little brothers and sisters while I practice. I wouldn't be able to juggle seven flaming boatswain pins at once without her help! And Ebano here"—Cerisse thumbed toward the gangly man in his mystic robes—"wouldn't even be able to speak our language if she hadn't tutored him. Besides," Cerisse tossed out, "I can't stand thinking of you and Belen alone. In the woods. The cold . . . dark . . . woods."

"Cerisse! Ebano! Have either of you ever camped out in a forest? There are monsters there, and snakes, and poisonous plants—all sorts of dangerous things." Jace struggled to think of more, but ran dry. "You might get hurt—or die!" The more he tried to convince them to stay, the more he started thinking maybe this whole thing was a bad idea. Best to stop that line of thinking right now.

Cerisse puffed out her chest in mock anger. "My mother is a Qualinesti elf. I was born to run around in the woods. And Ebano traveled here from Far Kundalaria."

"Oh, he did not. You and I both know that's just what Worver says for the crowd during Ebano's act! There's no such place as Far Kundalaria."

"Well, he came from somewhere, and he's here, so he must have traveled somehow."

Ebano stared down at them, barely noticing that the

conversation centered on him. Jace groaned and shoved another shirt into his backpack. The excitement of spending three days alone with Belen was dwindling right along with his temper. "Ebano." Jace tried to reason with the tall, thin mesmerist. "How did you get here? How . . . here?" He tried hand signals. Sometimes, those helped.

"Walked." Ebano smiled serenely. He flexed his fingers, letting each knuckle crack in a sharp sequence like softly exploding popcorn. "Walked the sands. Walked stone. Traveled the underworld. Now, go with you. Yes."

Jace rolled his eyes. "I can't talk either of you out of going with us?"

" 'Going with us?' " Belen's bright voice from the doorway made Jace duck and look around Ebano's shoulder. She stood in the sunlight with a small bundle at her feet. "That's a wonderful idea! Are you really?"

Jace groaned. No use now. What might have been a wonderful, romantic trip through the forest was now turning into a big sleepover. Cerisse hugged Belen while Ebano peered down his overlong nose at Jace's scowl.

"Of course we are." The half-elf juggler smiled. "We aren't going to let you perform without a net." The reference made Jace wince.

Despite herself, Belen smiled. "Thank you. There's a mystery to be solved, and it means a lot to me that you're willing to help me find out what happened. I can't stay here like this, even if Mysos would let me."

"What do you mean? Was someone mean to you? I'll—" Jace bristled. Cerise elbowed him and he gasped. She offered a quick apology and mumbled something about the wagon being too narrow, and Jace let it go.

"No, just the opposite." Belen continued, swallowing hard. "Everyone was very nice, offering me water or a place to sit, asking how I was, telling me that they don't believe the accusations or that they'd never let the White Robe take me anywhere against my will. Old Fodger, the escape artist, offered to teach me how to get out of wrist ties. Magical Marvin the Marvelous, the one who saws the girl in half, told me that if I needed to disappear he knew just the place. Really, they're being very nice." She hesitated, picking at a loose thread on her sleeve. "Pitying, but nice. I expected people to be afraid of me once they heard the rumors."

"What, that you're a dragon?" Cerisse grinned. "Are you kidding? That's good for business! Worver must be dancing in his wagon right now at the thought of all that good, hard steel pouring in once people find out. We'll put it up on all the signs. The Amazing Celestial Circus of Light has a real dragon! That'll pack them in!" She smiled, but then the edges of her smile faded. "That is, if you're haven't decided that you're too good for us, now that you're reptilian royalty."

Although Cerisse's tone was teasing, Belen paused and cocked her head to the side. "Do you think that?" she mused. "Do you think dragons believe they're better than anyone else? I don't feel better. If anything, I feel smaller than the rest of you. At least you know who, and what, you are. If Mysos is right, I'm not really human at all." She held up her hand and squinted at it. "I'm something strange."

"Maybe he's wrong. Did you ever think of that?" Jace asked, tucking the flap of his bag closed and tying the strings tightly together. "Maybe Mysos is crazy, and you're just a herdsman's daughter with a gift for dancing. Don't let that wizard's arrogance make you think he's knows everything."

"I guess." Belen's face pricked into a thin smile.

Jace took her shoulder. "Are you all right?"

She sighed. "I will be, once we find something to prove that I'm innocent."

"If we don't find something, we'll make something up." Cerisse poked her head up from her pile of belongings, tossing a pair of socks into her already bursting travel sack. "Don't worry."

"Cerisse!" Jace thumped the cot, shaking some of her

loose items down on her. "We can't just invent evidence and give it to the White Robes!"

"Why not? He's not coming with us. How would he know if we did?"

"He's a wizard. He'll find out," Jace said.

"Aha." Cerisse shook her finger at him. "So your problem isn't using false evidence, it's getting caught?"

"Wait, I didn't say that!"

"Close enough. Don't worry." Cerisse winked. "I'll handle it."

"Cut it out, Cerisse. We won't have to make anything up," Jace said between gritted teeth. "Belen's innocent."

"I'm sure she is, whether or not we find something to prove it. Therefore, ta-da and va-voom, we will find something, even if we don't find anything. You trust that she's innocent, right? So no matter what, we come back with something that says so."

Cerisse's argument was pretty good. As much as Jace hated to admit it, the goal was to prove Belen's innocence. After five years, any evidence that might have been left behind was probably long gone, and they might have to resort to less than honorable methods in order to prove that Belen wasn't responsible. As long as Belen really was innocent, what was the harm in creating "evidence"? Lying was better than coming back empty-handed and letting

Mysos take her away. Still, it didn't feel right. "We'll see when we get there," he said finally, shirking the whole thing. He didn't have to think about it now.

Belen shook her head. "I'm glad that you trust me, Cerisse, but what if you're wrong? What if I *did* hurt a lot of people and I just don't remember it? I don't know much about dragons, but I do know they are very powerful. If a dragon is angry, who knows what harm it could do?"

"Belen, you aren't the kind of person who would—" Jace started, but she cut him off.

"I'm not that kind of person *now*. Who knows what kind of person—or dragon—I was then? I might have been very different." She crossed her arms and narrowed her eyes. "I might have been mean."

"Hard to imagine, Lady I-Don't-Even-Like-To-Step-On-Bugs." Cerisse chuckled. "Don't worry. Even if you turn mean, Jace here will snap a whip and hold up a hoop for you just like Worver does when he's taming the lions. He'll do anything for you. It'll be fine." Jace felt his face flush at Cerisse's teasing. And he was going to have to spend three days in the forest with her? He'd wring her neck before it was over!

Belen rolled her eyes. "Thanks, Cerisse, that's a wonderful image. Will the circus be keeping me in a cage and feeding me raw meat as well?"

"Why not? Might improve your temper," Cerisse teased.

"Be serious!" Belen thrust her fists on her hips, glaring.

"I am! Well, partly. Look, Belen, nobody can see the future. Not me, not Jace, not even . . . well, maybe Ebano can, but nobody understands what he's saying. We'll just go and see and worry about it then." Cerise dug under her bed for a few more things, overturning her footlocker to shove the last of her stuff into an already filled-to-the-seams bag. "Back to business. I don't need my tights or my heavy juggling hoops. Do you think I'll need these rubber balls? My silk scarves, I'll definitely need those—oh, and my bandoliers . . ."

Giving up on the half-elf, Jace turned to face the tall mystic. Ebano Saham stood at the center of the whirlwind, tapping the ends of his fingers together. When he saw Jace staring, the willowy man smiled and made a graceful gesture.

"Ebano, are you even going to pack?" Jace asked.

"Pack?" The mystic stared at him, uncomprehending.

Jace sighed and tried again. "Pack, Ebano. Clothing in bag? To travel?" He mimicked the action, holding up his knapsack. "You know?"

"Ah." Smiling, Ebano folded his arms into his sleeves

and bowed slightly. "This one saw stars moving, writing on the sand of forever. All things one, all place here, all time now." He nodded, reciting the lines as he'd been taught and leaving Jace even more confused than before.

"Ebano, what does that mean?"

The mystic's purple eyes sparkled. "Packed before."

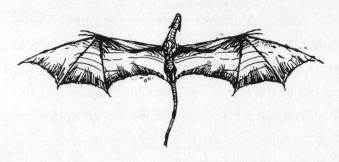

CHAPTER FOUR

he woods were dark and cold. A rich fall wind pressed the branches and tossed the hems of the circus folks' traveling cloaks. The four of them had left the circus heading south around noon, and by dinner time they'd found a small path with a broken sign marking the way to the village. Jace knelt to brush the dirt away from the placard with one hand. "Angvale," he read, looking up again at the faded path. "This must be the road to the village."

"Not very well traveled, is it?" Cerisse pushed back some thorns and creeping vines that had grown over the edges of the path. "This must have been wide enough for wagons once, but now there's hardly room for us to go one at a time."

"The correct path is not always the easy one." Ebano fluttered one hand behind Cerisse's ear and pulled out a violet. He handed it to her with a bow.

Jace shook his head and sighed.

"At least it's clear enough to travel." Belen's voice was soft, hardly rising above the whistle of wind. She looked up at the scraps of gray, cloudy sky visible through the rustling branches of the tall trees. "We should hurry. It looks like that storm will start soon, and we'll need a place to camp out of the rain."

Cerisse went first, the others following her sure-footed steps. Slowly, the storm gathered, bringing the false twilight of gray clouds. "Mysos said that there were still ruins where the village stood. If we find them, maybe some of the buildings are in good enough shape to provide shelter.We can start our investigation in the morning, when it's drier."

"Is that going to bother you?" Jace asked Belen. "Staying in the village?"

She shook her head. "I don't feel anything here, Jace, other than nerves. No memories, no flashes of insight. Nothing. It's as if I've never been here before." Ahead of them, Cerisse pushed aside a long, tangled spray of vines falling from a low-hanging tree limb, and Belen suddenly fell silent. There, beyond the brushy limb, lay the fallen village of Angvale.

Beyond, the moss-covered stubble of small buildings lay nestled among rocky outcroppings in a lovely forest dell. The houses had been made of gray stone, with thatched roofs and thin cobblestone steps leading from one to another down twisting, soft loam paths. A little brook with an arched stone bridge marked the center of the village square, where the people might have held market on sunny days. Even ruined, the village still held a certain beauty. Today, however, the storm blotted out the sun and made Angvale look somber, spoiled, and a little bit eerie.

The walls of the buildings had been torn apart, roofs pushed over as if by some mighty wind. Through the remnants of the thatching, long rend marks could be seen, as if a row of four massive swords had slashed through wood, straw, and all. The paths were ruined, both overgrown and caved in by a great weight pressing down on them. The stone bridge had fallen to the side, foundations crushed and waterlogged by the little stream. The unmistakable marks of heavy, clawed footsteps were etched into the stone terraces of the dell, despite time and the moss's efforts to reclaim them, and entire houses were misplaced, wrapped around the bases of ancient trees by the icy wind of a dragon's breath.

Not a creature stirred, nothing broke the silence. The village was completely empty.

"Oh, wow." Cerisse stepped out into the dell, her form illuminated by a flash of lightning. "A dragon really did attack this place."

Jace steadied himself. It was one thing to hear about a dragon attack—quite another to see the aftermath, even years after the event. He could almost hear the screams of fear, the swoop of a dragon's wings, the rush of wind from a fearful breath. Could that really have been Belen?

Cerisse trotted over a low, ruined wall and into the village proper, eagerly investigating the strange town. "Cerisse, be careful. Some of those buildings are unstable," Jace warned. She didn't answer, but continued on, making a soft sound of delight at some small object found within one of the huts.

"Cerisse?" Jace repeated, louder now. The wind had picked up and was whistling through the low, mossy out-croppings around the village. Something bothered him. "Be careful."

"I will!" Cerisse climbed like a mountain goat over the various ruined buildings, poking first in one and then another. "Look, a church! No, it's not a church. What is it?" Curious, she vanished down the path. "I'll be right back."

"No, Cerisse! Stay close—we don't know what's out there. Cerisse?" Jace called. "Gah, I don't think she heard me." He turned around to gather the others, but stopped short when he looked back to see if Belen had followed.

Belen had gone as white as a sheet, her gray eyes wide and stunned. Her breath was labored, heavy in her throat

46

as she looked from side to side at the wreckage. She walked forward and touched the broken foundation of the nearest building, her hands pausing in the etched scar left by claw on stone. When she spoke, her voice was soft and strangely flat. "There was a watchman standing here with a lantern. I don't know why he had a lantern. Dusk hasn't settled yet. The lantern caught my attention. I remember the flickering light—the lantern, the sunset, the fire in the sky. Scarlet and orange in the clouds." Her lips twisted into a scowl as if she were baring her fangs, her eyes far away. Her voice changed, falling to a whisper. "They won't see the strike coming. I will be quick."

A crack of thunder rumbled in the sky, and Jace jumped. When he looked back, Ebano stood beside Belen, his dark hand on her shoulder as she trembled like a leaf in the storm. "Come in from the west. The sun behind me . . ." Belen murmured, barely aware she was speaking. Ebano shook her gently, and Belen blinked and fell a staggering step forward against the wall. "Oh!" Her eyes flashed open, and she caught herself. "By the gods," she said. "I *was* here. I don't know . . . I don't remember much . . . flashes, really. Just images. Nothing specific."

"Of being a dragon?" Jace asked gently.

"No, just of the village. I don't know!" Belen exclaimed. "I remember hearing people scream, and a lot of chaos—but

I feel sad, and angry, and panicked. My heart is pounding like a parade drum. Dragons shouldn't feel that way, right? Dragons are powerful. If I was one, why would I feel scared?"

"Scared?" Jace prompted.

Belen nodded, wiping her eyes on her sleeve.

"You might have been a villager here." Jace tried to make himself believe the words, to forget the look on her face when she'd been describing the attack. "Scared" was the last word he would have picked to describe it. He wanted to help her, take her in his arms, and reassure her that it was all right, that he'd protect her no matter what. Jace puffed up his chest and fumbled for the words, managing only a squeaky, "Are you going to be all right?"

"I'll be fine," Belen said softly. "I just need to sit down."

Beside Belen, Ebano tightened his hand on her shoulder and looked at Jace. "Inside." His voice was low and echoing as he struggled for the words. The mesmerist gestured at the ruins ahead as a few large drops of rain splashed on the broken cobblestones. "Rain soon."

"Right. The storm." Jace shook himself. "Ebano, help Belen. I'll find Cerisse and see if there's a place up ahead that can give us shelter." He waited until Ebano gave him a nod, and then hurried ahead.

The town was a shambles, with ruined buildings dotting the terraced landscape. The one building that was still whole stood at the center of the town's plaza, just beyond the little bridge over the babbling brook. Jace scrambled over the broken bridge and through the windswept plaza, avoiding a large muddy patch of old-turned earth where it looked like something—probably one of the massive old trees—had been torn up and tossed away by a powerful force. The standing structure at the end of the plaza was twice as tall as the other buildings would have been and wide across the bottom, standing on a thick foundation of cut stone. The windows were of colored glass, though dim with dust and the waste of several unattended autumns. The heavy oak door was solid—and slightly open. He called Cerisse's name again and heard her yell a response from inside. Picking up his pace, the tightrope walker headed that way.

Cerisse smiled at the sight of him, gesturing him over. She was turning over several battered books on a broken and tilted desk. "I think this was a school," she said, waving him toward her. "Look at these books and the little desks all around. The chalkboard even has writing on it—a bit—though it's pretty faded and smeared." Cerisse looked around with friendly interest. "I think they were doing mathematics, before—"

"Before they died?" Jace snapped. He regretted the words as soon as he said them. "I didn't mean it to sound that way . . ."

Cerisse set the books down. "Good thing Belen's not here to listen to you talk like that," she said. "I thought you said she was innocent?"

"I do!" he protested. "I . . . did. I don't know what to think now, Cerisse. When she came into the village, she recognized it, and there was something terrible in her eyes." Worried, he sank down to sit on the edge of the broken desk.

He'd expected a snarky comment or some kind of biting remark, but Cerisse sat down beside him and placed her hand on his knee. "Don't worry. If she was here for the attack—dragon or no dragon—it had to be traumatic for her. One of our theories is that she was the dragon and was tricked into coming here. Maybe we were right. Or maybe she was a girl turned into a dragon by a horrible curse or some dark magic. In either case, she'd be pretty shaken up to be back here, right? Seriously, Jace, you give up too easily." Cerisse peered out the open door, signaling to Ebano, who was coming slowly down the broken path. "All the signs point to a pretty bad storm tonight. I'm glad this building is still standing."

"Yeah." Jace was glad to change the subject. "I wonder why? All the others were pretty badly ruined."

"Maybe the dragon thought there were children in here and didn't attack it."

Cerisse's idea inexplicably cheered Jace. If that was true, then maybe the dragon that attacked the village wasn't doing it to hurt people. Maybe, even if it was Belen, she'd had enough control of herself not to really go all out. But if that was true, and she hadn't hurt them, then where had all the people of the village gone?

Ebano helped Belen up the stairs into the stone school, and Jace took her hand so she could lean on him as she stepped across some brambles growing at the door. Belen smiled kindly and squeezed his hand, then looked around at the little building. The sky outside had turned so dark that every flash of lightning appeared to rip through the clouds, like light needles darting black cloth. Jace shivered. The wind had turned colder, and the rain—once drips and drops—was sincerely coming down.

He closed the door as best he could, but the brambles that grew against the doorstop and along the stairs were thick and hardy, resisting Jace's best efforts to pull them free. Belen bent by one of the desks, picking up overturned, ruined books and setting them on the little pew beside the table. "What's this?" she said, holding something up. It was moldy and crushed, but had been protected from the elements by the books that had lain on top of it, and it was unmistakably familiar.

"That's a pinwheel." Jace walked over and took it from Belen's hand, turning it this way and that to examine the coloring. "Look, the maker's mark is still on it—hey! That's our circus's mark, see here? The Amazing Celestial Circus of Light."

Cerisse looked over his shoulder, frowning. "You're right. Now that I think about it, the circus used to come through this area a lot, so we might have been here. But we stopped traveling this far south because Worver said the area wasn't populous enough. Not enough audience to justify the trip." She strode over to the door and peered out into the growing darkness as if trying to picture the town in its heyday. "I think I might remember this place after all—but it sure didn't look like this back then. There were banners, and the village square was different. Something's missing in the middle, like a big statue or something. Probably got torn down in the dragon attack."

Jace had forgotten that the half-elf, despite looking the same age as him, was actually several years older due to her heritage. Of course she'd remember more clearly than he did. "Maybe there was a tree that's been ripped up?" Jace voiced his own suspicion.

Cerisse shook her head. "No. Something smaller." The half-elf cocked her head and stared at the village through squinted eyes. "I remember now! Wow, it has changed. This village was bright and friendly. Lots of children." She sighed. "I'm glad we're here to find out what happened. I hope we can and make things better. In fact"—she smiled at him—"I'm sure we will." Leave it to Cerisse to juggle the facts around and make it sound like coming to this ruined town was a great idea.

Light flared in the school behind them. Ebano hummed a pleasant sound of approval, pulling pages from the old books and using them to feed a small fire he'd built up near the front of the room. Grateful, Belen pulled closer, tugging her cloak around her and sitting on the stone floor near the little blaze. She looked pale, wan, her lips thin. She sipped a cup of tea that Ebano had heated at his fire, and said little to the others. They ate a little, huddling around the warmth of the flame, the silence broken only by the faintest attempts at conversation.

Thunder crashed around the little schoolhouse, rain rippling through the streets and moving like snakes in steady streams over the broken cobblestones. Lightning flashed through the treetops, casting stark shadows on ruined foundations and the wreckage of torn-apart roofs.

Jace blinked. One of the shadows had moved.

"Cerisse," he said quietly. "Did you bring those juggling daggers?"

She was lying on one of the wooden student pews, eyes half open like a cat's. They gleamed in the firelight. "Yeah." She stretched, sitting up to gaze past him. "Why?"

"Get them out. I think—"

He had no time to say more. Thunder shattered the silence and shook the walls of the schoolhouse, making dust trickle down from mortared stones and high wooden beams. In the plaza, two more shadows detached themselves from the fallen stones of ruined houses, heading toward them with an odd, ungainly lope.

"The fire"—Cerise had seen them too—"it's gotten the attention of some forest animals. Probably bears."

Jace fell back, wishing he had some way to bar the door. "Those aren't bears." He drew his weapon—a short sword left to him by his father—as the door flew open. It wasn't wind that had nearly torn the door off its hinges, though. It was a monster.

It stood taller than any of them, on rear legs much like a man, but it was covered in shaggy, tangled fur. Fangs like knife blades curved down from its long, wolfish muzzle, and sharp, short claws cut the air at the end of five agile fingers. It walked with a hunch, as though the muscles of its back were foreshortened to allow it to walk on all fours.

But its rear legs, bent like an animal's, still carried all of its weight forward to allow those sharply clawed hands to lash out at Jace. Feral, maddened eyes gleamed from beneath the dark strands of fur, boring down over the creature's long muzzle with eager glee. It stepped forward, crashing into the room with a snapping series of barks. Jace could see three more like it in the ruined square running half like wolves and half like men.

"Werewolves!" Ebano shouted from the lighted area by the fire. He began scrambling around, digging through his pack. "Need mantano!"

"Mantano?" Jace stared, shocked. "What does that mean?"

"Mantano! Mantano!" The mesmerist yelled again. "To fight . . . mantano!" He clearly didn't mean the werewolves, so it must be some kind of weapon. If only Jace knew what the word meant!

"I don't understand you, Ebano!" Jace shouted, dodging again. These werewolves were fast. "What are you trying to say?"

Ebano struggled to find the equivalent word in their language, eventually giving up. "No bite! No bite!" He crossed his hands, waving them in the air in a gesture of negation.

No bite? I can manage that, Jace thought, darting to

the side as the creature struck out at him. Can't promise as much for those claws, though.

The beast swung again, its massive muscles flexing, driving the sharp-pointed hand forward. Jace ducked, shifting quickly, and plunged his sword into the beast's side. Not enough to kill it, Jace guessed, but enough to injure it badly. With any luck, the monster will just leave, licking its wounds.

Luck wasn't with him. Roaring, the beast slammed both hands down on Jace's shoulders, shaking the boy with a massive, bone-rocking jolt. Jace's blade fell from his hand. The monster snarled, its lips twisting into a sickening grin, and snapped its jaws together eagerly. Jace looked down at its wound, the red tear along the beast's side where his sword had struck it—and he felt his hopes shatter like glass.

The pink, bloody edges of the wound were closing, sucking themselves together in a smooth motion like wet mud oozing together after parting it with your foot. Within three breaths, the creature's side had healed to little more than a red, angry slice. "We definitely have a problem," he gasped under the weight of the creature's palms.

Three small daggers, the size of throwing darts, flicked past his ear in a sudden buzz of motion. The creature staggered as they pierced its shoulders and throat, pushing the beast backward. A fourth pinned the monster's arm to the heavy oak door, piercing flesh as well as fur.

Ducking swiftly out from under the creature's arms, Jace struggled free. He spun and ran back to his friends, scooping up his short sword as he sped past. Cerisse stood, legs wide for balance, in the center aisle of the schoolhouse, two more daggers already in her nimble hands. Behind her, Ebano had spread one hand wide to push Belen back behind the fabric of his purple sleeve. His eyes were wide and alight as he muttered soft words in his chirping tongue, his left hand making a warding sign in front of his strange eyes.

One of the windows of the building shattered, and Belen screamed. Another of the thickly furred, hunched monsters crashed through the fragments of flying glass, landing with a heavy thud on the stone floor. It stood gingerly, shaking tinkling bits of glass from its fur. Jace could see that this one, too, was healing, the lacerations in its side sealing up as long glass splinters fell to the floor. He could hear a third scrabbling at the rear of the building, trying to find another way in. Soon enough, it would follow the other and make its way into the room. There wasn't much time.

Jace looked up. "Rafters!" he cried.

Cerisse followed his gaze, identifying the same safe haven that Jace had seen. The rafters were thick oak in good condition, but higher than these heavy monsters could jump. Even if they stood on the pews, the werewolves wouldn't be able to reach them. The only problem was, how would they get up there?

"All right, Jace, it's worth a try. You pitch, I'll loft!" She sheathed her daggers in an instant, checking her belt for their traveling rope while Jace jumped up onto one of the nearby pews. They'd need the extra few inches.

"Go!" he called to her, cupping his hands together and lowering them down to his ankles.

He tried to concentrate on Cerisse, who was running toward him full tilt with the ardent excitement of a performer. At least she wasn't scared. The monsters had caught sight of her, and while the one at the doorway pulled Cerisse's dagger from its arm, the other gave chase. Cerisse didn't notice—or didn't care—and barreled forward, leaping up to place her foot in Jace's laced fingers with a perfectly timed jump. He hurled her upward as hard as he could and watched her feet vanish into the air above his head. "Got it!" she cried, catching hold of the rafter with both hands and swinging on it like a gymnast. She pulled herself up onto the flat oak above and started tying her rope to the wood.

"Stellar!" Jace grinned. "Now—"

Unfortunately he'd forgotten that Cerise was being

chased by a four-hundred pound creature made entirely of muscle. The werewolf bowled him over, knocking into the pew so hard that it cracked in half. Wood, Jace, and fur landed all tangled up on the floor. Jace rammed his short sword into anything that didn't feel like oak, twisting about to recover his footing beneath the weight of the beast.

The second one must have decided that Jace was too small for two of them to eat, because he dropped Cerisse's dagger on the floor and charged straight for Ebano and Belen. Belen stepped back, lifting a thick piece of pew in both hands like a club, but Ebano never lost his serene smile. The mesmerist continued to wave his fingers back and forth, clicking his tongue over strange syllables as the werewolf plunged toward him with arms lifted wide over its head. Ebano lifted his chin and stared the beast squarely in the eyes. "Be still," Ebano intoned, snapping his fingers three times. The monster jerked, its howl choking into a mangled squawk, and froze.

Jace managed to wriggle free, feeling his clothing tear under the vicious claws of the werewolf rolling on the ground with him. It outweighed him by more than three times as much, but he was faster and had a trained acrobat's dexterity. Scrambling over the ruined pew, Jace hurled it into the creature's face and rolled back until he felt the wall behind him.

Before it could shake off the wreckage, a long rope dropped, uncoiling only a foot in front of Jace, right down to the floor. "Climb!" Cerisse yelled.

"But Belen and Ebano—" he started.

She cut him off. "Later! There's a seven-foot walking werewolf who wants to eat your face, and that pew isn't going to stop him! Ebano's fine. You're not. Now climb!"

Jace didn't need to be told a third time. He grabbed the light silk rope and jerked himself upward. Hand over hand, as quick as a cat, he scampered up toward the rafters. The werewolf, now free of its entangling wooden planks, jumped for the rope. Jace felt its hot breath against his ankles as it leaped to bite at his legs, but the werewolf fell short. Jace flipped himself upside down on the rope, twisting his ankles around the top portion to keep them safely out of the way of the foaming beast below. With a few more tugs of his legs, Jace pulled himself up to the rafter, took Cerisse's hand, and swung aboard.

"We have to get them up here." Jace looked down at the mesmerist, who was still standing by the fire between Belen and the frozen werewolf. The third creature was climbing through the broken window now, and more had begun to pull open the door and pour in through the front.

"I don't think we have to worry about that." Cerisse

clung to the thick rafter, her grin shining in the dim light. "Look."

Ebano wrapped his arm around Belen's waist and drew something from his belt with a flourish. Belen clutched her makeshift club with one hand, grabbing him with the other. Ebano snarled, holding the frozen werewolf's eyes with his own. Then, with a loud command in his native tongue, he flung his hand downward and a burst of brightly colored yellow smoke exploded at his feet.

The smoke engulfed them, breaking the hypnotist's hold over the frozen werewolf. It howled in delight, crashing forward into the drifting waves of color—and found nothing.

"Nice trick," Cerisse muttered. "Where are they?"

"Look with your eyes," Ebano intoned with the aplomb of a practiced stage performer. "See with your heart." He was standing on the wooden rafter behind them, holding Belen by the waist and smiling like a cat that had gotten into a fisherman's net.

"How did you—"

"What was that—" Jace and Cerisse burst out together. They stopped and laughed, clinging to the heavy oak rafter high above their enemies.

Below them, more and more of the werewolves poured through the door and the broken window, circling and snapping at the air. The thunder outside rocked the building once more, shaking the walls with its rolling echo. The fire that Ebano had started on the floor sputtered, but the wolves did not approach it, keeping a respectful distance even after the blaze died. The only light in the room came from lightning that flashed outside the window. Jace clung to the thick oak, staring down at the pack of vicious creatures. Fear fluttered in his stomach. The height didn't bother him, but the sight of all those teeth and claws, well, that wasn't the kind of net he wanted to land in if he should fall.

Just then, lightning shattered the darkness outside, flashing through the windows. Jace caught sight of a smaller figure in the doorway. It stood draped in a fluttering cloak instead of heavy, thick fur. The thumping as the thunder passed wasn't that of padded feet, but instead of a heavy staff upon the floor, coming in from the heavy rain.

"Is that Mysos?" Jace whispered.

"No," Belen answered through gritted teeth. Her eyes were better in the darkness than Jace's, or even Cerisse's, if she could make out the solitary figure surrounded by the ever-moving pack of werewolves. "It's a woman."

Light flared again, and Jace thought at first that it was another bolt of lightning. But then the flash stayed, bursting through the room in a sharp spread of cold bluish white light.

Belen was right. The woman now stood in the center of the room. She was dressed in rags that wrapped around her thin, wicker-frame body. She held on to a staff that was little more than a torn and ravaged tree limb, with knots and broken bark marring the length of the wood. Her gray hair, mussed and laced with greenery as though she'd been sleeping in the musty woods, was twisted into a knot at the nape of her neck. Her eyes were wide and rolling, brown as mud surrounded entirely with white.

"Starlings in a tree." She spoke in a voice as dry as burning twigs. "Come down, little birds, and—" Her voice fell and her eyes widened as her gaze fell upon Belen. The mad old woman clutched her staff with both hands, baring her teeth amid the howls of the wolves around her.

"*You.*"

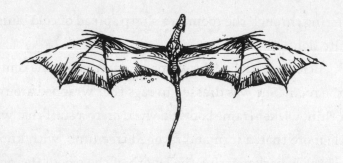

CHAPTER FIVE

You dare return here after the woe you've caused, the lives you've ruined?" The ancient woman stomped her staff upon the ground, the hem of her tattered cloak and skirt swirling around brown, earth-stained feet. Anger radiated from her slight form, shaking her shoulders. "You return here only to die—you, and all those who come with you."

"You . . . know me?" Faced with such deep hatred, Belen struggled with the words. Jace saw her knuckles whiten around the heavy oak rafter, her face paling before the woman's threats.

"Who, whom you have ruined, would not?" the forest hag spat. "We would never forget your face, Belengithar—no matter how you try to hide in sheep's clothing."

"We?" Jace seized upon the word. "You're a survivor of this village—are you implying that there are more like you? Others who lived through the attack? We need to find them, ask them what happened. Belen doesn't remember anything—"

"And I want to make this right," she cut in, "to help anyone who was hurt. But I need to know where they are to do that."

"Where they are?" Cackling, the old woman spread her hands wide. "They are here! Look upon them, dragon and friends of dragons! See the people you have cursed." The werewolves howled and snapped, leaping toward the ceiling in desperate attempts to catch anything that hung too low. "You did not just destroy this village in your attack, Belen. You left its spirit in as much rubble as its houses, rent and broken."

"The werewolves?" Cerisse gasped.

"Yes, the wolves. But they are not true werewolves. The moon holds no power over them. They are cursed wolves, the entire village forever condemned by Chislev, cursed for their failure." Her red-rimmed eyes stared. "I will tell you the story before you die, yes, I will, so that as the wolves strip the flesh from your bones, your last thought will be of her great betrayal." She smiled, and there were black holes between her teeth. "This village was once blessed by the goddess Chislev, and even after the gods left this land in the great Cataclysm, we always felt that her power remained among us, however silent, however soft. We knew this because

Chislev's hands remained among us. The forest stayed green and warm through the winter, our butter was always sweet, our streets clean. We protected the stone at the center of our village—a stone sacred to Chislev—and we had peace.

"Then *she* came." Snarling, the old woman stamped her staff on the ground once again, knocking aside one of the broken pews. "From the sky, without reason, she brought a rain of ice and hail where there had only been warmth. Her claws pulled down the village, ripped up the houses, tore away the stone. And for what? We did nothing to her—nothing. We left milk on the doorstep and sacrificed the first hunt each winter to the great silver dragon of the forest. We revered her—and she destroyed us. Chislev's grace fled this village, and we were cursed for our failure to protect the sacred stone."

Ebano said something in his strange tongue, muttering as if he were trying to muddle out some of the details. He tugged on Belen's sleeve, catching her attention, and she turned a stricken gaze to him. "Not kill?" he asked her, trying to make himself clear. "Belen not kill?"

"Hey, that's a good question." Cerisse raised her voice to shout down over the noise of the wolves. "Did Belen kill anyone? Or are they all werewolves?"

The hag scowled. "Minus a few lost to hard winters, the wolves number the same as the villagers once did, yes."

Cerisse brightened, and Ebano sat back on the rafter. "You didn't kill anyone, Belen! That's great!"

"Great," Belen muttered, looking down at the vicious creatures beneath her feet. "Yeah."

Jace called down to the hag. "Why were you immune to the curse?"

"I was cursed as well, though not the same as the others." She snarled at him. "I did not lose my human form because someone had to tell the tale. Someone had to take vengeance on the one who did this to our village! I was the priestess of the stone, I who told the seasons by its shadow and prayed to Chislev, even after others had forgotten her name. So did my mother, and her mother before her. For my failure, I was given the task of recovering the sacred stone, though my powers were stripped and my body withered. Chislev is angry. She will have vengeance on the one who stole the stone. I will give Chislev vengeance, and then, perhaps, she will lift her curse. Even without magic, I will call on the villagers who were cursed by my failure, and they will seek vengeance for me."

The old woman stretched out a withered finger. "Even dragons can die, Belengithar, and your friends will die with you! You can't stay up there forever. Your food and water are down here with the wolves. You've no fire and the night is turning very, very cold." The rain outside pounded on the school windows, blowing through the main chamber with the shivered breath of ice.

"I don't think she's going to compromise," Cerisse muttered under her breath. Jace tended to agree. The woman didn't seem sane, and living with all these wolves probably wasn't helping. Plus, there was the village's curse.

"We have to find a way out of here." Jace frowned. "Belen, any ideas?"

The wind shifted her silver hair, tickling her serious expression. "We can't fight. I don't want to hurt them, even if they're attacking us. I'm glad we didn't cause them any harm when they first attacked." She peered around the room. "If we could make it across these rafters to the wall and then down through the window, we might be able to escape into the woods."

"Then what?" Cerisse shook her head and her auburn braid swung below the rafter where she lay. "We get chased through the woods at night, in the storm, by around three score of wolves? How does that make us safe?"

Belen frowned. "Well, I hadn't exactly planned on going with you." All eyes riveted on her, and she flushed. "She's after me, right? And the wolves . . . she won't let them chase you if I'm still here. Once you're outside and safe, you can find a way to come back in and save me, maybe in the morning when the wolves start to sleep."

"I don't like you risking yourself, Belen," Jace said immediately, and Cerisse rolled her eyes. He ignored her and continued. "What if Ebano uses one of those smoke bombs—"

Ebano rolled his fingers out from his palms. He quoted another of Worver's lines: "Keep in safety that which you care for most."

Exasperated, Jace asked, "What does that mean?"

Ebano pointed down at the wolves. "Bag," he said simply.

"You left them in your bag? Great." Jace sighed. "Not a lot of options, then. We all head for the window"—he stressed the "all"—"and Belen waits in the rafters while the rest of us get out into the woods. We'll find weapons or a way to draw some of those wolves away from the school building, and then come back for her."

Cerisse slid to her knees on the rafter and began to crawl. "Ebano, tie this rope around your waist, and then we'll tie it to each of us—Jace and me—so that if anyone falls, the other two can hold him up. Does that make sense? No, no, don't turn the rope into a snake, Ebano, that's wonderful, but now's not the time."

Jace and Ebano followed her, with the mesmerist between the two acrobats. Although this wasn't Ebano's forte, the gangly man had the reach to pull himself from one rafter to another, and his balance wasn't bad. The wolves beneath them jumped and ran in circles. Some paced back and forth beneath Belen, and others simply remained where they were, eyes glittering in the light. Belen was right, Jace admitted to himself. They wanted her.

But that didn't mean the wolves wouldn't kill them all if given a chance.

Swinging Ebano by the rope first, they burst out the window in a quick flash of motion. They fell more than fifteen feet through the broken glass window to the wet ground below, cracking shoulders and rolling in the muck to try and shed the impact of their fall. Ebano, having fallen the shortest distance, was the first on his feet. He untied the rope binding them together. By the time he tugged Jace to his feet they could hear the werewolves baying behind them.

"Run!" Jace said it and did it all in one breath. Several wolves raced out the front door of the school building, and others jumped to the sill of the window, ignoring the glass that cut their feet. "Stay together!"

They raced through the darkness and the ruins, ducking from one hiding place to another as the wolves followed their path. Where he could, Jace stopped to harry the beasts, using his sword to cut them as best he could before darting away again. He could see Cerisse doing the same in the darkness, throwing rocks to slow their pursuers or to cause echoes of a false trail that led the wolves away. Ebano followed, his steps silent. Despite the blinding sweep of rain that pelted down from the heavens, Jace thought they were making good time through the village . . . until they turned a corner and found themselves facing the plaza and the schoolhouse—again.

"The wolves are herding us like sheep," Cerisse gasped, brushing water out of her eyes.

As she spoke, two of the massive werewolves blurred in from the shadows to the right, their faces contorted in feral smiles. A third, smaller figure—probably a woman— slunk along the wall of a house on the other side. "They're flanking us," Jace warned the others. He tightened his grip on his short sword and tried to remember that these beasts were—had once been—human. "Don't kill them," he growled.

Cerisse stared at him as if he were insane, four daggers twisted in her fingers. "Kill them?" she spluttered, rain slicking her red hair. "We'll be lucky if we can hurt them!"

Ebano straightened, pressing his palms together in preparation.

The first one charged. It roared toward them, jaws open, claws extended, and met with the tip of Jace's sword.

Although the acrobat wasn't the finest swordsman in the world, his reflexes saved him more than once in the wolf's attack. It could see better than he could in the darkness, but he was faster, and the rain made the muddy ground shift, another benefit for Jace.

The boy wheeled, striking out behind him with the sword. It caught the wolf on the shoulder, scoring a bloody mark that would soon close. The creature struck again, howling. Jace leaped, drawing his feet up and allowing the werewolf to swipe beneath him. The claws nearly hamstrung him, but Jace was faster, and pulled his sword beneath him so that it thrust down beneath his feet. Using gravity and his agile grace, Jace slammed down onto the wolf's back, sword first. The creature screamed and fell, crumbling to the ground. He knew that it would be on its feet again as soon as its wound magically healed, but at least for now, he'd won. It only made the moment a little less glorious that four more were circling just at the edge of his blade.

He could see Cerisse climbing on the second were-wolf's shoulders, dodging its flailing arms nimbly as its mouth snapped at the empty air where she'd just been standing. Ebano was using his mental powers to still the third, though the darkness made it difficult. Jace could already hear more beasts in the shadows, coming closer with every breath. He tried to ignore them, blocking the werewolf's strikes with quick thrusts of his short sword. It was getting easier to see his opponent, its snarling fangs whiter, and its eyes gleaming in the . . . firelight?

"Jace!" Ebano's voice rose over the ruckus. "The school!"

He hadn't noticed the glow start, flickering at the edge of his vision while his attention was taken up by the werewolf's attack. Jace twisted past the wolf's lunge, trying to look where Ebano was pointing. His eyes fixed on the one standing building left in the square. The school was on fire.

"Oh my gosh!" Cerisse cried, legs flailing from the wolf's shoulders. "She's going to kill Belen! The hag said that Chislev would have vengeance. Belen can't get out of there without the wolves tearing her apart—and if she stays inside, she'll burn to death!"

On the stairs of the building, a shadowy figure with ragged robes and a staff guided the wolves out, cheering on the fire with mad laughter.

"We have to help Belen!" Jace tried to get past the werewolf, but it blocked him and threw him backward to the ground, leaving thin gashes across his chest from the tips of the its claws. He was lucky it hadn't caught him more fully, or he might be looking at his stomach inside out. He leaped to his feet and tried again, but there were more wolves around them, slipping through the ruins, over the broken walls. The fire grew higher and higher, sweeping quickly up under the eaves toward the roof despite the pounding rain. It cast racing shadows of wolves all around, on the walls and the plaza square, flickering in the lightning and dancing over mud and stone.

It took a moment to recognize that one of the shadows was neither human nor wolf. It pressed from within the church, stretching out darkly against the flame, roaring in an echo of the fire's hunger. With a breath, as thunder once more split the sky, the roof of the building exploded into shards. Stone crumbled as if struck by a mighty blow, and the wolves howled in rage and fear.

A tremendous head, as large as the horses that pulled the caravan wagons, rose within the flame. It shone as bright as fire-forged metal, sparkling and shimmering amid the heat of the blaze. The neck and wings that flared out against the sky were silver, swordlike, crested, and they swooped with glittering, metallic luster. The creature bellowed with rage, and ice swelled from its breath, mixing into the rain to form a long cone of cold, glittering sleet.

"Dragon!" Cerise choked.

"Belen!" Jace screamed.

Ebano only smiled.

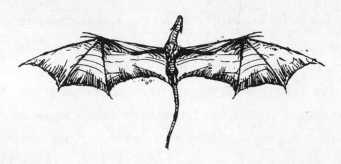

Chapter Six

The massive dragon rose above the burning school, braving the thunder and lightning of the downpour with a resounding clarion cry. The wolves that surrounded the plaza fell back in surprise. Jace could hear the old hag's voice crying out, trying to rally her servants, but chaos was overtaking the ruined village square. Jace felt a stab of panic followed by a warm glow. Belen really was a dragon!

She was even more beautiful now than she'd ever been before. Terrifying, yes, but beautiful. Her scales shone like molten steel in the firelight, her eyes wide and filled with righteous anger. Wings like silken sails unfurled behind her, catching the firelight and reflecting it back in a mirrored prism to illuminate the dark smoke that rose from the building below.

With a buffet of her wings, the dragon rose to her rear legs, stretching out her neck over the square. She released another blast of cold dragon breath, snuffing the worst of the flame beneath her. Jace could see the werewolves leaping up to savage the dragon with their teeth and claws, but they did little more than scratch at her heavy silver scales. The ring of claw against metal echoed amid the clamor of thunder. The dragon—Belen, Jace forced himself to acknowledge—snapped at them, catching one in her teeth and hurling it aside against the broken stones of the village. It got up a few seconds later, healing swiftly and limping away. Many of them started fleeing, frightened by the massive jaws and swift swipes of the dragon's feet.

"She's going to kill them!" Cerisse cried out.

The silver dragon roared, spreading her wings and stepping out from the wreckage of the school building. The old woman stood her ground, clutching her battered staff despite the wind of the dragon's beating wings and the rain. Around the hag, wolves began to scatter, raising howls of terror into the night. Watching the scene, Jace imagined he could see the night five years ago when the dragon landed amid the village. Villagers had screamed and scattered like the wolves, unable to defend themselves against her rage.

The dragon arched her neck, eyes wide and dark. Lightning flashed, illuminating her sharp ivory fangs as she bent toward the old woman in the center of the plaza. Jace could hear the hag shriek, "By Chislev, you will not hurt this village again! I will give my life to stop you!"

The wolves around him had already fled back into the shadows, their eyes wide with haunted memories of the dragon's first attack. Cerisse was right behind him, and Ebano strode a short distance beyond. Cerisse yelled,"We have to stop her! Belen, don't hurt these people!" A single stroke of the dragon's tail, one strong buffet of wing or swipe of claw could tear down a building, much less kill the woman who stood before her in those ragged robes. Belen's head swept forward, and the old woman dropped her gnarled staff.

"Oh! She's going to bite the hag's head off!" Cerisse gasped.

Despite the fact that Jace privately thought it would serve the woman right for setting the school on fire, he couldn't let Belen do it. But they couldn't get close enough to stop her in time, and the whipping wind and crashing thunder drowned out their shouts. The dragon struck out with her fore paws, blocking the hag's retreat first to one side, then the other, drawing her claws closer and closer together around the old woman until she was caged in. The old woman screamed, terrified, and stepped back within the cage of the dragon's claws. She prayed to Chislev in gasping breaths. Belen's head sank down until it was only an arm's length from the shivering old woman. The dragon's silver lips curled, revealing vicious-looking fangs. Jace could see the lines of panic etched on the old woman's face, her white-rimmed eyes wide with horror.

"Fear not, forest warden," the dragon said softly, and Jace could hear the echo of Belen's voice within the words. "I shall not hurt thee"—her eyes narrowed—"though you would have taken your vengeance out upon my companions when your anger is with me." The old woman huddled back and cowered low to the ground, shivering at the dragon's anger. "Whatever happened here all those years ago has been stolen from my mind. I have no memory of attacking your village. I do not remember your blessed stone. My mind has been erased. But this I know: I wish to help you, not harm you."

"Lost your memory? Ha! Just like my wolves—the villagers. They know nothing but the hunt and the forest now, that and a terrible need for revenge. The stone has cursed them. I think it has cursed you too, for your arrogance and greed, stolen your memory so that you cannot enjoy your victory." The old woman rose, shaken, snatching her staff off the ground and clutching it close. "You brought this on all of us!"

"Perhaps I did. Perhaps my actions were as terrible as you say. For my part, I cannot say. But no matter what has occurred in the past, I am here now to make amends and bring what peace I can so that we may all heal. This was no victory. It was a tragedy—for us all." The dragon's long silver tail coiled about her feet, hiding the sheen of perfect steely claws. It was hard to believe that this was truly Belen, though something in the dragon's grace and poise spoke of Belen's dancing, and her steady gray eyes held the same soft strength. The dragon stood in the stone plaza, keeping her claws spread in a fence around the shuddering, huddled forest hag that had defied and threatened her.

Summoning her courage close like the rags she pulled tight around her shoulders, the hag faced the dragon despite her quavering knees. "Return the stone, dragon," she spat. "Only then can you repair what you have wrought."

The dragon shook her head gracefully. "I do not have your stone. Whoever has done this has wronged us both. In either case, I will return it to you if it can be returned. You have my word on that."

"Your word is worth nothing to me or to this village. Your death would mean more," the old hag spat.

The dragon settled her shoulders lower, her neck bowed. The she uncurled her claws and set the woman free. "Go." The silver dragon raised her shining head, folding her wings back against the sinuous length of her body. "Care for the people who have been cursed by this misfortune.

We will speak again." The dragon drew in a deep breath, lifting her head to release a gust of snow and cold wind that soared above the village. Snow fell all around them from the blast, icing over the last of the fire and driving the monsters farther into the forest.

The old woman staggered out of the dragon's grasp. Two faithful wolves slipped out of the shadows of ruined buildings, crawling close enough to tug worriedly at the hem of her ragged robe. At another roaring cry from the silver dragon, the old woman turned and stormed away, one hand on her withered staff, the other twined into the fur of one of the werewolves.

The dragon's snow fell, cold and white, throughout the village. It hung in the air, shadowed the ruined walls, and turned the storm into a hazy drift of cotton. Belen stared up at it, watching it fall. She was frozen like a statue amid the drifting stars of ice. As the wolves slid into the shadows, baring their teeth but afraid to risk the dragon's wrath, the village fell into silence. Even the voice of the storm slowed and quieted, the thunder muffling its voice into a hesitant peace. The school's fire turned to smoke and ash, and a few crumbling boards fell from the wrecked ceiling. Jace stepped onto the plaza, the stone beneath his feet wet and slick, and stared up at her. The dragon was magnificent, glowing with strength, power, and grace, her gray eyes bright and cold. Cerisse and Ebano came up behind him, gazing at her with awe and wonder.

Belen lowered her head, closed her eyes, and lifted her wings above her shoulders. She gave a little shake as if she were casting away the faint fluff of snow that had landed on her broad shoulders, and her form dissolved in a shimmering wash of magic. Her scales shone briefly as they turned to soft skin and silver hair. Her size was simply no longer epic, drifting like melted ice into a woman's slight form. Only a soft breath later, Belen stood before them as calm and recognizable as if she'd just stepped off the third ring of the circus into the shelter of the velvet curtains backstage.

"Belen," Jace said, trying to keep his voice from shaking. "Are you all right?"

She nodded. Cerisse reached out and took her hand as the light glittered on tears frozen to the dancer's cheeks. Belen squeezed her fingers gently. "I'm fine. I didn't think it would be"—she paused and cleared her throat—"easy."

"Turning into a dragon?" Cerisse looked back at the ruined schoolhouse.

"You were in trouble. The building was burning. I knew I had to do something, and then I just . . . did."

"Large problems require large solutions." Despite the tired cliché he quoted, Ebano's voice was soothing in the darkness.

The storm was passing, the clouds gently opening here and there to allow moonlight to reach through the forest leaves. Snow from the cold dragon's breath still trickled down, slinking through the shadows of the ruins in pale memory of the wolves that had fled the dragon's wrath.

Belen tried to smile. "For a moment—when I changed form—I remembered something. I did attack this place. I know I did. But I didn't steal the stone, and I didn't kill anyone." Her voice had the ring of certainty.

"I've been thinking about that, you know," Cerisse said.

"What, while you were fighting the werewolf?" Jace said, grinning.

"Yes, actually. Unlike boys, I can do two things at once." The juggler pouted for a moment, shaking her head so that her auburn braid wagged past her waist. "I think I know why Belen attacked the village—sleight of hand." The other three stared at her, confused, and Cerisse continued in a huff. "Oh, come on! It's obvious. She didn't steal the stone, did she? Well, if she didn't, then someone else did. What's the best way to move something big without anyone noticing? Distraction! It's the oldest trick in a magician's book."

"Dragons are very distracting," Belen said seriously, drying the last of her tears.

"They are! And best of all, you wouldn't even have to hurt anyone. All you had to do was cause a ruckus—and then they'd take the stone. Of course, whoever it was didn't expect everyone to turn into cursed werewolves." Cerisse frowned. "Nobody I know could trick a dragon, though. It's a lot harder than one of Ebano's mind tricks, or Worver's fluffy shell games. Maybe a wizard . . ."

They all paused, considering the same thing without saying it.

"It's possible," Jace said at last, trying not to shiver in the cold. He wiped the blade of his short sword clean and resheathed it. "But there wouldn't be any proof here, would there? None that we could find, anyway." The black scar in the ground where Chislev's stone had stood was dark despite the touch of frost that layered the ground elsewhere.

"Whoever did it," Belen said, stressing her uncertainty, "would have had to convince me to attack. Threaten me," she said, "or offer me something I couldn't refuse." She struggled to remember, releasing Cerisse's hand to rub her temples. "I don't know! It seems so foolish. Why would I endanger all these people? Why would I hurt so many innocents?"

Ebano took her arm, gazing down at her. "So sad, dragon girl," he clucked. "You are stream."

"I think the cold's gotten to his head." Jace shivered,

wishing just a bit that the school was still on fire. At least that would have been warmer. "He's not making any sense."

"Stream?" Cerisse shook her head, making strange, exaggerated gestures as she spoke. "We . . . don't . . . under-stand . . . you, Ebano!"

"He doesn't know the language, Cerisse, he's not deaf," Belen snapped. She turned to Ebano and searched his eyes. "What do you mean, Ebano? Stream? What are you trying to say?"

Ebano smiled and bent down, sketching a wavy line in the frosted earth. "Stream," he said. "Belen stream." He pointed at her, and then tapped the line. "Here." He pointed at the top of the line, where he had begun the drawing. "Belen," the mesmerist said again, reaching up to grasp her hand and pull her down. He placed her palm over the area, pressing it against the earth. "Belen here."

"What is he saying?" Belen stared, puzzled.

It took three breaths for Jace to realize Ebano's message. "The beginning! That's what he's saying. Streams don't just come from nowhere, Belen, they have to start somewhere. Whoever talked you into doing this, whether it was blackmail or a threat, must have been able to find you before you came to the village. This had to start some-where! Can you remember if you had a home somewhere? A cave . . . or . . . or . . ." He fumbled. The idea of Belen living in a cave was preposterous, but he had no idea where dragons tended to live. "Maybe a tower?"

"I . . . I remember a mountain surrounded by forest. The sun was setting behind it when I flew to the village." Belen's mouth dropped into a little O. "It must be to the west of here! Once it gets light, I could fly in that direction until we found it."

Ebano looked animated as he stood and helped Belen up. Jace chuffed the taller man's shoulder, congratulating him as Cerisse pulled Belen into a hug. "Er, that is if I can remember how to fly." Belen sighed, engulfed by the eager half-elf's premature celebration.

They passed that night amid the ruins, finding a spot that had been sheltered enough by a fallen roof that they could crawl beneath it and stay dry. Ebano managed a second fire, and they warmed tea by the flame when the cloudy morning sky turned pink and orange. Belen walked away from the others and stood in the plaza, staring at the scar in the earth. Jace left her alone, struck by how much the image called up the memory of the dragon staring up through the snow toward the stars. He could hear Ebano and Cerisse chattering, communicating in a strange dance of words and gestures, and laughing when they couldn't understand what the other one had said.

Jace wondered how long it had been since this ruined

village had heard laughter. He looked up toward the west and tried to imagine the spread of silver wings against a blazing sunset. She'd probably come right through that gap in the trees, snowy breath flaring in great sweeps of mist and ice against a sunset sky. Jace shivered despite himself, imagining the terror of the villagers in the face of such an attack—even worse, to feel a curse take hold, changing their form and erasing their minds so that they remembered nothing but the feral, animal existence of wolves. Was that worse than losing the hundreds of years of memory that Belen must have had, being a dragon? The feeling of power, the deep mysteries of magic and enchantment that were native to such noble creatures, all of that was lost to her, shed like a cloak on a warm day.

Did she feel small? Did she feel unbalanced, standing on two legs instead of four? Did she struggle to remember the feeling of her wings against the clouds? Standing there, staring at the torn ground where the stone of Chislev must have stood, did Belen have any memory at all of what the village looked like before she tore it apart?

What was she thinking, standing so very still?

"Belen?" Cerisse called from the campsite. She was standing over the ashes of their little cooking blaze, knocking the charred wood over with her boot, burying the signs of their fire. "Sun's full up over the edge, even if you can't see it through the forest. Ebano told me that he doesn't sense any more storm in the sky. Well, he either said that or he said he wants to turn into a bird, I'm not sure. But I think the wing thing means he's ready to fly." She turned warm brown eyes on the girl in the plaza. Behind her, Ebano twisted his thumbs together and flapped his fingers up and down on either side in good imitation of a bird.

Jace walked to Belen's side and shared a smile. "Think you can do it?" She met his eyes directly, and Jace felt his heart skip a beat.

"Turn back into a dragon? Yes." She nodded. "I have that part figured out. It's the part that comes next I'm not so sure about—the flying part."

"Don't worry." Jace laid his hand on Belen's arm. "Cerisse and I are acrobats. We fall just fine. And as for Ebano, well, if you really want, we can tie him to your leg." Despite herself, Belen had to laugh. Ebano smiled, but Cerisse's mouth tightened and her eyes narrowed grumpily.

They gathered around Belen—not too close—while she shifted into dragon form. Once again, Jace watched the strange misty shiver of the air around her body, the feeling like a drawing in of breath as if the world itself pulled close about her form and draped it with silver scales. There was no stretch of flesh, only a quick blur of motion, like a magician's thin scarf passing before the eyes, coating her in silver and steel, great dragon's wings, and a massive, graceful neck that flowed and moved like the thick silk of her hair.

Belen lay down upon the ground, poising her foreleg so that they could easily climb up to her back. Jace and Cerisse managed it easily and helped Ebano along. The hypnotist settled his thick purple robes about him, muttering softly in his foreign tongue as he patted the dragon's scales. Running his hand along her neck, Jace noticed she was softer than he'd thought. The scales looked as hard and cold as metal shields, but they were soft to the touch, like buttery leather, and the thin ruff of silver hair that trailed down the back of her neck was finer than spider silk. "Everyone aboard?" Belen twisted her head around to look, and Jace gave her a thumbs-up.

"If you need to land along the way, feel free," he told her. "You haven't done this in a while."

"Don't worry, Jace. We'll be fine," she rumbled, stretching her wings. "You're not the only one who can work without a net."

Belen rose to a crouch, lifting her wings high. Although Jace and the others were ready, he'd never felt anything like the massive weight of force when Belen hurled herself up from the ground. A single pumping beat of her wings propelled them high into the air, over the trees and ruined buildings in a tremendous leap. Cerisse squealed in sudden panic, clutching Jace, and Ebano laughed aloud. Jace grabbed the silver frill in front of him and hung on for all he was worth. The world swung and pitched beneath them, then fell away to mist.

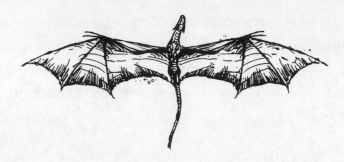

CHAPTER SEVEN

Flying on a dragon's back was a lot like the first time he walked alone on a tightrope, Jace thought, as the wind streamed in his hair. There was the rush of adrenalin, with one foot on a thin wire and one hovering a hundred feet above the ground, shifting in the winds of chance. Balance shifted unpredictably, tilting with each swoop of the dragon's wings. Sometimes, when Belen went down to avoid a gust of wind, it felt as if there were nothing keeping him aloft—but then, with a startling rush, gravity returned, and the thick solidity of the dragon's body lifted him up again.

Below them, the forest sped past in a blur of green and brown, trees and hillocks smearing together. He felt Cerisse's hands on his waist, and he heard her soft squeaks when the dragon suddenly changed altitude. Though he couldn't tell if Ebano was behind him, he hadn't seen any lumpy purple robes spinning to the ground below them either. He'd just have to hope for the best.

They'd been flying for more than an hour, sailing sometimes north and sometimes south along a western horizon as Belen looked for trees, hills, rivers—anything she might recognize. Occasionally she would turn in wide spirals, staring down at a particular landmark until Jace thought he'd fall off. Then Belen would straighten in the air with a cry and shoot off with renewed speed. She couldn't swoop beneath the trees as they were too close together, but occasionally she would fly so close to them that their uppermost branches smacked against Jace's boots.

Suddenly she cried out, the rich trumpet of the dragon's voice breaking through the rush and bluster of wind. She glanced back at them, snaking her head back and then forward on her strong neck and angling her wings to make for a tall ridge that rose out of the deepest forest. Jace strained his eyes, trying to see what had caught the dragon's attention. A tower rose from the top of the hillside, a tower unlike any that Jace had ever seen or even dreamed might exist. The tower's thick gateway was arched and turreted, wide enough for a dragon to walk among the beautifully carved stone. The tower itself was much taller and wider than a human habitation, rising on a massive foundation to admit a draconic body within the safe confines of its walls.

On first sight, it was beautiful: glittering white marble sheltered by clinging ivy and softly shimmering willow trees growing close to the base. But as they grew closer, Jace could see the signs of weather and wear. Silver banners, once long and fluttering, now hung in rags from the main turrets, and the doors stood open, blocked by a thick coat of dead leaves and fallen branches from the nearby trees. The trees were worn down, branches broken by storms, and the grass all around it grew long and wild with neglect.

"Did it always smell like this?" Cerisse yelled."Or do you think there was some . . . uh . . . food left out when she left five years ago?"

Jace frowned. Now that Cerisse mentioned it, there was a putrid sort of scent in the air. The fountain by the side of the tower was filled with stagnant water, brown with a thin veneer of moss and mold floating on the surface. As Belen swung wide around the tower to see it from all sides, Jace noticed more—ragged scratch marks in the earth near the front archway, spattered dark stains on the marble, and broken white fragments scattered on the ground, fragments that Jace was fairly sure weren't stone. "I think that while Belen was out . . . something moved in."

A roar from the inner rooms of the wide tower confirmed Jace's suspicions. As Belen completed her circle, he could see that the front courtyard was no longer empty. Crawling out of the shadows from between the heavy doors of the marble spire was a creature nearly half the dragon's size. It had the body and head of a massive lion, furred and tawny, but no lion ever had wings like a bat's, nor a second goatlike head that rose from the left side of the creature's shoulders, and a third, terrible red-scaled dragon's head to the right. The scaled and serpentine tail lashed around the monster's rear legs.

"Chimera!" Ebano's voice was barely audible. "Very bad!"

Jace gulped as the creature launched itself into the air. The lion's head roared in anger, and the dragon hissed as it lashed on its scaly neck. Belen tilted to the side, wings slicing through the air. The chimera was quick to gain altitude, and quicker to turn and spin to chase her, its lighter body more flexible and speedier in the air. "I can't land or set you down," Belen growled, and the rumbling in her chest shook Jace's legs. "We'll have to fight."

They had no time to disagree, for the chimera was attacking.

It opened its dragon head and a thin stream of liquid fire blazed past them. Startled, Belen jerked to the side, wings lifting to protect her passengers. The fire struck the delicate leather, burning it with a hiss. Belen yelped in surprise, twisting in the air and forcing Jace and the others to cling to her back. She faced the chimera, claws extended, and attacked the lighter creature with a vicious swipe. The chimera rolled like a barrel, slipping out of her grasp, and charged them again before she could recover from her attack. Jace could swear the goat's head was laughing.

Two daggers flew past Jace, swishing through the air to land with twin thunks in the chimera's shoulder. The impact caused the beast to miss its lunge, and it flinched past Belen's head. The lion's head roared in anger. As it passed over Belen's back, the dragon head lashed out at them, catching Cerisse in the arm with its vicious bite. She cried out and tried to smack at it, but was too slow. The chimera recoiled before she could hurt it.

As the dragon swung about for another pass, Jace tried to see how bad Cerisse was injured. Her arm was already swelling up, the skin purpling. She tore a piece of cloth from her cape and started wrapping the wound. "Are you all right?" He couldn't stop staring at it, horrified at her injury.

"Fine!" Her voice shook. "Just hang on!"

Unexpectedly, Belen twisted in the air, turning sideways to the ground, her wings pointed straight up and down. Cerisse cried out, grasping onto Belen's strong wing bone, and Ebano clung wholly to Belen's back. Jace, who had been turned around, had nothing at all to grab hold of, and felt himself slipping to the side. He spun against gravity, trying to grasp for Belen's silvery frill as he felt himself sliding into free fall, and managed only to grab the ridge of her back. The chimera swung past overhead, its claws scoring Belen's shoulder only a few inches above Cerisse's head—right where Jace had been sitting. The knock of the creature's strong forelimbs broke Jace's grip.

Belen righted herself the instant after the chimera passed. Jace slammed into the dragon's right foreleg and scrabbled to find a handhold on the slippery scales. Cerisse's hand swung down, and he grabbed it instinctively. His hand grasped her wrist, her hand clenched around his, and Jace hung there, hundreds of feet above the swirling ground. Staring up, he realized belatedly that she'd done it with her injured hand. Cerisse locked her fingers onto his and pulled with all her might. "I won't . . . let . . . you . . . fall!" she screamed into the wind, half out of desperation and half out of pain.

Ebano grabbed Cerisse's waist and gave her leverage, but it wasn't enough to allow her to pull Jace aboard again, not with the poison eating away at the strength in her arm.

Realizing that Jace was in danger, Belen tried to swing the other way, tilting her body so that he would swing forward onto her shoulder, but the chimera had looped around again and was plunging down from a high dive. The beast's dragon head snarled, flames flickering at the corners as it prepared to launch another gout of fire. If Belen stayed at this angle to allow Jace to climb back aboard, the chimera's fire would burn her stomach. If she turned to protect herself, Jace would face the full brunt of that flame—and almost certainly die.

Jace steadied himself. The ground below him spun, and the chimera was swinging close, ready to attack, close enough to reach. Gripping the silken frill at the dragon's neck, Jace planted his feet on the silver scales at Belen's shoulder. He didn't have time to count to three as he usually did before stepping out onto a tightrope. He had time only to make sure Belen saw him, and then he jumped.

Jace ran out onto the dragon's wing, keeping his weight light against the fore bone. The wing bone under his feet was wider than a tightrope, but slicker and rounded where the rope always felt solid and hard. Nevertheless, walking on shifting slopes was Jace's forte. He had no moment to balance or prepare himself, but hurtled down the dragon's wing toward the chimera as if he were racing beneath the big top's heavy canvas. Step after step, Belen's wing tensed under his weight. He was nearing the first joint now. After that the bones became much thinner and less capable of carrying his weight. He was going to have to jump.

Images of his last time on a tightrope flashed through his mind. Faces spun again beneath him, and the sick jolt of the rope as it slid under his foot. Jace pushed it all away. If they were going to have any chance of defeating the chimera, he had to reach it. He had to leap from the dragon's wing to the chimera's and be aboard the beast before it knew what was happening.

Jace looked up into the chimera's horrible dragon maw, the flames licking around its gums and teeth, and launched himself into the air. Wind rushed past, tugging at his hair, his clothes. Jace tried not to think of the ground swooping past far beneath him. One second. Two. Three, and there was the chimera's outstretched wing!

He landed lightly, barely tapping it with his toes before pushing off toward the creature's back. The chimera screamed, gouting flame where Jace had been and nearly scorched its own wing in the attempt. Jace was already three feet farther in, almost to the creature's shoulder. Luckily, Jace thought as he reached out to grab the lionlike mane, the creature was almost certainly too stupid to just—

Roll. The chimera twisted in the air, abandoning its attack on Belen. The wings clamped in close to the body, the lion's head roared wildly, and the beast spiraled over onto its back. They were dropping through the air at a sickening speed, the tail of the creature hissing up toward Jace like a stabbing spear. He managed to avoid it and clung tightly to the chimera's back, driving his short sword between the shoulder blades. The wounded chimera screamed and began to right itself—and that's when Belen struck.

The act of rolling to try and unseat Jace had opened the monster's belly to the mighty silver dragon, and with no other way to save her friend, Belen drove forward. Her claws sank into the creature's skin, tearing at flesh and bone alike. The chimera screamed in anguish and spouted flame at Belen and her passengers, but the heavy wind of her wing beats kept them safe from the fire. Taking advantage of Belen's attack, Jace reached up, grabbed hold of her claw, and swung himself over the chimera's shoulder and onto her foreleg. Belen let go of the wounded chimera, thumping her wings furiously to slow her fall, and Jace clung for dear life.

The beast fell, goat's head braying, lion's head yowling wildly, and dragon's head spouting a twisting gout of useless fire. The chimera spun through the air until it struck the ground below with a crunching sound that made Jace's blood run cold. The monster lay silent upon the hillside outside the tower.

"Jace, are you all right?" Cerisse screamed, peering over Belen's side. Her face was like a small white moon beyond the dragon's beating wings. Jace stared up at it, wondering if he'd ever seen her look so pale in all his life. It must be the poison from her injury that made her look so terrified, he thought.

"No!" He gulped, trying not to remember the sound of bone breaking on earth. It reminded him too much of his father . . . of the day . . . that moment when . . . "Get us down!"

I hate falling. I hate falling. The words rang like a mantra in Jace's mind. What had he been thinking? He could still feel the absence of solid foundation, the sense that there was nothing between him and the ground. And then, that sound . . .

Belen landed swiftly, curving in a wide spiral that brought them quickly to the earth outside the silvery tower. The chimera's body had fallen just inside the inner courtyard, crushed by the weight of the fall. Cerisse leaped from the dragon's back and flung herself at Jace, hugging him with all her strength. "You did it!"

"It wasn't just me." Jace untangled the half-elf from his neck. "Everybody helped."

"True. But you were the bravest." She beamed, gasping back tears.

Jace tried not to think of the sick feeling in his stomach, and attempted to smile.

Once everyone had dismounted, Belen changed form

again, slipping easily from mighty dragon back to slender girl. She crossed the courtyard and stared down at the dead chimera, sorrow etched on her face. "I didn't want to fight it," she said softly.

Ebano took her hand and smiled sympathetically, but Cerisse was the one who gave voice to what everyone was thinking. "You didn't have a choice. It would have killed us." She let Ebano tut-tut over her arm, smearing the wound with a particularly vile-smelling paste and binding it gently with a piece torn from his purple sash.

"Yes, but it was just an animal that had found a home in an empty tower. The chimera was just defending its territory." Belen's shoulders fell.

"I don't think so." Jace interrupted her.

"What?"

"I don't think that chimera just moved in here randomly," Jace said. "I think that the curse affected it too. That stone's absence sickens everything it touches—the villagers, your memory, and now this creature. Everything that's gone wrong here traces back to it."

Belen considered this for a moment and then nodded. "You might be right. The hag said that the power of the stone affected the whole forest—and this tower is within the forest's heart." She shook her head sadly, turning away from the body of the dead beast. "It's likely that the creature was once an innocent pet or a keeper of this tower charged to protect it while I was away." She pressed a hand against her forehead. "This whole thing is such a tragedy."

"Do you think that whoever stole the stone knew what they were doing?" Jace asked. "Can anyone really be that evil?

"Evil is a serpent's tooth in the heart of man." Ebano's comment was unprompted, and startled them. The hypnotist's purple eyes were soft, sweeping up from the creature's torn body to stare at each of them in turn. Ebano struggled for a moment to come up with one of his rote fortune-telling predictions that seemed to fit, and then said hesitantly, "Man does not think of others when he follows his heart. Let your heart be your guide." Although the words were out of place, Ebano meant them earnestly, conveying all the meaning and sincerity he could through his eyes and delicate hands.

A sad stillness followed his words. Cerisse, ever irreverent, was the first to break it. "Wow. For someone who doesn't know our language, Ebano, you can sure turn a phrase."

Ebano smiled, gesturing toward the horizon. He moved his hand over the forest first, then lower, sweeping over the creature's body to encompass its death. Reciting his fortunes in a somber tone, he intoned another of his memorized babblings, "Grain by grain a loaf, stone by stone, a castle."

"All right, now we've lost him again." Jace chuckled, patting Ebano on the back. "Don't worry, Ebano. We'll figure it out on our own." Ebano shook his head and said something in his native tongue, clicking his teeth over the syllables. Unable to understand, Jace turned to Belen. "Ready to go inside?"

She shuddered. "I don't think it's going to be pretty in there."

Belen was right. The main chamber of the lower tower was roomy and had once been well decorated, with couches, bookcases and tables, a large fireplace, and other comforts, but now, it was ruined. The chimera had not been a tidy guest. It tore down the tapestries to create a rotting bed in the corner and left scraps of old feasts on the floor. The stench was almost enough to make Jace climb to the ceiling to get away from it, but he compensated by holding his arm to his face to bury his nose in the fabric. Belen seemed less affected by it, ignoring the smell as she knelt by the pile, pulling one of the tapestries out far enough to look at the grime-stained picture on the fabric.

"Belen?" Cerisse caught their attention on the far side of the massive chamber. "I found a set of stairs that leads up. I think they're too small for the chimera to use, and they look dusty."

"That means the upstairs might be in the same condition that it was on the day I left five years ago." Releasing the tapestry, Belen stood and crossed the room. "If there are any answers in this place, they're up there." She gave Jace a faint smile, and his heart leaped to see it. "Let's go find them."

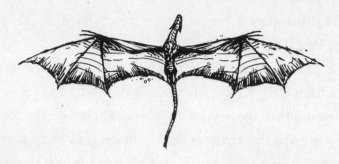

CHAPTER EIGHT

Despite the tower's size, there were only two floors. The first, as Jace had seen, was roomy and had been plush, possibly meant for a dragon to sit or curl up comfortably. The ceiling was high and well reinforced. The second story, at the top of a long, coiled set of stairs, was smaller, built for a human-sized occupant. The top floor was divided like a wheel into three wedge-shaped areas by wooden walls. The first area, where the stairs emptied, was obviously a small study and library. There was a mahogany desk, ornate but still serviceable, made of fine dark wood with lighter details. Shelves of books lined the walls, along with trinkets, bric-a-brac, and other odds and ends to give it a homier feel.

Jace picked up book after book, brushing the dust from the spines. "History, history. Oh, look." He traded it for another. "Another book on history. Hey, Belen, I never knew that you were so interested in the past."

She tried to smile, tapping her forehead. "Apparently, I got over that."

They all shared a laugh, then spread out to look through the room. There were doors in the two interior walls, one to the north and one to the east. Ebano opened the north one, then reddened. He pointed, turning his face away, and Belen looked past him.

"Bedroom," she chuckled. It seems I wasn't very tidy."

Cerisse was tugging on the other door, the one that led to the east. "I think this door is locked. Belen, can you remember how to get in?"

Belen was sifting through the paperwork on the desk. "I don't think so. Nothing here is bringing back any memories."

"Not at all?" Cerisse tugged on her auburn braid thoughtfully. "Maybe you didn't live here?"

"No, I think I did. It's not unfamiliar, it's just not . . . I can't put any memories with it." Belen held up a half-finished letter. "This is my handwriting. But I don't recognize the name of the person to whom it's addressed. Then there's this half-finished manuscript. It looks like I was writing a book." She tossed the papers back onto the desk grumpily, and a few fluttered down to the floor. "There's nothing about the stone, the village, or any reason I might have attacked them."

"Maybe there's something in here?" Jace walked over to the eastern door, checking the lock that had confounded Cerisse. He twisted the handle, and it moved freely—but the door didn't open. There was an audible click as the metal moved about in the latch, but he couldn't budge the portal. "It's not locked," he scowled, leaning into it with his shoulder. "It's jammed. The door's broken."

"Broken?" Belen and Ebano clustered around the door. "Look," Belen pointed. "The hinges are melted shut."

Jace squatted and took a closer look. "Those aren't melted. They're *frozen*. The metal's gotten so cold that it fused together. Normal ice can't do that. It had to be magical. Like—"

"Dragon's breath." Belen's eyebrows knitted together.

"Can we break down the door, Jace?" Cerisse pushed between them, peering at the door.

He contemplated it for a moment, and then shook his head. "I don't think so. That door's solid oak, the hinges are steel—that's expensive stuff!—and set into a stone wall."

"What about turning into a dragon, Belen?" The half-elf looked hopeful.

"In here?" Belen blinked. "I'd squish you like bugs, and my mass would probably knock down half the tower."

"Oh, right. I forgot how big you are in dragon form."

Cerisse chewed on the tip of her thumb, trying to come up with another solution. Jace chuckled. Cerisse was really sweet—when she wasn't being so annoying. It was too bad she was such a tomboy and wasn't more graceful, kinder, less frustrating—all the things that pretty girls were supposed to be. Cerisse was pretty, Jace had to admit that, but she wasn't . . . well . . . she wasn't Belen.

Ebano shooed them away from the door, the purple arms of his robe fluttering. "Little door," he said, clucking at them. "Little. You see."

"Uh . . . is he going to do magic?" Cerisse asked Jace out of the corner of her mouth.

"Either that," he chuckled, "or he's trying to make us feel better."

Ebano pulled a piece of broken chalk from his pocket and began drawing on the door. He drew intricate patterns, circles inside circles, and delicate knotwork all along the edges of the door in three different colors of chalk.

After about a quarter of an hour, Jace started reading one of the history books. Cerisse had abandoned the effort long before that and vanished into Belen's bedroom. Jace could hear her tidying things in there, organizing them by their weight and heft, if he knew the juggler as well as he thought he did. Meanwhile, Belen skimmed over the bookshelves, lifting pieces of art and staring at each one in turn. Every time she put one back on the shelf, she let out a little sigh as if she'd been holding her breath while she balanced the trinket in her hand.

Then, just as Jace's patience was about to break, the eastern door cracked, a sharp bark of sound. Jace whirled to find Ebano with his eyes closed, hands palm out on the door—which was shaking. The wood quavered and slammed back and forth within the doorway, the patterns quivering with every energetic shake of the wood. Ebano lifted his hands from the door and brought them together with a booming clap.

The door shrank.

Wood ripped away from frozen hinges, tearing from the steel with a quavering shriek. The door dwindled, first by inches and then, with a pop, in a shocking rush. As it opened, a cold gust of air hissed out from the room beyond. It was dark in there, without windows or other doors to let any light inside. The floor was crusted with a thin layer of ice, and the walls were patterned with spiderwebs of glittering crystalline frost. A damp wind fluttered past, raising the hairs on Jace's arms and sending a shiver down his spine. "What's in there?" he whispered.

Belen took a step forward, standing in the doorway. "I don't know."

"Was this where you kept your food? To keep it cold?"

Cerisse bobbed her head over Jace's shoulder, ducking back a bit.

"Dragons don't eat cold food," Belen said, leaving Jace to wonder what they did eat. Belen shivered and rubbed her hand over her arm. The goose bumps rippled her flesh visibly, and she stared into the room. "I don't want to go in," she said suddenly, a helpless note in her voice. "Something's very wrong. There's something terrible in there. Something awful . . ."

"It's all right, Belen." Jace brushed her shoulder, his other hand ready to reach for his sword. "Whatever was inside, I won't let it hurt you. You don't even have to go in first. Cerisse, step inside and see if you can see anything."

Cerisse shot him a wounded glare. "Go in yourself, you big jerk," she muttered.

"Wait. Something happened here . . . something that hurt." Belen was struggling for words, searching her memory for the events that caused her pained feelings, but Jace could see that she had little to go on.

"Perhaps you were attacked? Did someone break in? Did you lock them in there?"

She hesitated, trying to remember. "I don't know. But I can feel it—whatever's in there, it hurt me. I feel almost"— Belen took a deep, shuddering breath—"afraid."

If Belen had a bad feeling about this . . .

"We don't have to go in there." Jace tried to sound encouraging.

"Yes, we do." She glanced back over her shoulder at Jace, and then took a hesitant step forward. "Even if it hurt me then, even if it's going to cause me pain now, I have to go in. I need to know what happened. If not for my sake, then for the sake of the village of Angvale. I can't leave them to live in the woods like feral animals, their village in shambles. If I did that to them, then I had a reason. And I think the reason is in this room." She took another step, then a third, slowly entering the cold, dark room.

Jace would have stopped her, kept his hand on her shoulder, but Cerisse gently pushed him back. "Let her go," the half-elf whispered. "She'll be all right." Whether it was some instinct that made Cerisse hold him back or whether she read something on Belen's face in the shadowy arch of the doorway, Jace didn't know. But her tone of voice was so serious, the earnest look in her brown eyes so rare and unexpected that he stopped dead in his tracks.

Ebano stepped close to Jace in the doorway, carrying an ornate candelabrum with three half-melted candles in its twisted brackets. He'd lit them, and now he held up the light so that the soft glow illuminated the room beyond the ruined door. The room inside was smaller than any of the others at the top of the tower. It was barren—no furniture, bookshelves, or any sign that someone might live within. Instead, the walls were slick stone covered in frost, and there were no carpets at all.

The only thing in the room was a flat piece of thick ice, square around the edges but curved in the center, like the old worry stone Jace used to rub while he watched his father walk the high wire. Soft furs, now old and crusted with ice, had been piled around the strange slab of ice. They were scattered on the ground around it, stiff and frozen in discarded lumps. Belen walked toward the stone stiff legged and knelt on the cold ground by the side of the slab. She reached out with one trembling hand and touched the furs, and they crackled beneath the pressure of her fingers.

"Was this another bedroom?" Cerisse inched forward through the door, marveling at the icicles that decorated the ceiling beams. "Did you sleep there sometimes, on the stone? No, it's too cold for a human, and too small for a dragon, that can't be right."

Belen didn't answer. Jace followed Cerisse, heading deeper in while Ebano stood in the doorway with the candles in his hand. Ice crunched under Jace's feet. When he reached Belen's side, he saw that she looked as if she'd been struck by a physical blow. Belen ran her hands along the inner curve of the ice and choked back a sob.

"Belen, what's wrong?" he asked her without thinking.

Then his eye caught the shape of the indentation, and the evidence fell together into a single blinding insight. "By all the gods," he said, his voice breaking as he stared in mingled horror and surprise.

Cerisse was the one who said it out loud. "The crevice in the ice. It's shaped . . . like an egg."

"They took it." Belen's voice was flat. Her eyes sparked like bright chips of cold ice, and her hand drifted to the center of the depression in the stone. "They took my egg. My child! Stolen!" Her body shook, and her mouth snarled into so fearsome a grimace that Jace could have sworn she'd grown fangs.

"Belen remember?" Ebano murmured, a deep sympathy in his tone.

Belen surged to her feet, hands clenched into tight fists. "I do remember! I was asleep. I'd slept for almost a year, waiting for it to hatch. Something woke me, and when I checked on the egg, it was gone. Stolen! Betrayed!" Jace was shoved back, struck by her shoulder as she rose, and her strength was enough to knock him over. He landed on one hand, frost crunching beneath his fingers as she lost herself to the rage.

"Someone came in while I was sleeping and stole it. Only one village knows where I live. They must have taken it!" Belen was lost in the resurfacing memory, speaking to people who weren't really there. "You have my gratitude for awakening me, and telling me where to find my egg. When I return, you will be . . . well . . . compensated." Belen's knees gave out beneath her, her voice falling faint. Her eyes closed, tears brushing her eyelashes in small, frozen crystals.

"I remember now," she whispered, slowly coming back to reality. "That's when I left—for the village."

Cerisse rushed forward to grasp Belen's wrists, keeping the silver-haired woman from collapsing. "Belen!"

"I wasn't alone when I awoke. Someone was here," Belen said softly, rage turning to sorrow. "They woke me, told me that the village stole my egg. That's why I went there—to get it back. That's why I attacked Angvale."

"And while you were fighting them, someone stole the stone." Jace picked up one of the castaway furs and wrapped it around Belen's slender shoulders. "We were right. You were set up. They say that the good dragons' eggs were stolen by the evil dragons to make their horrible draconians for the War of the Lance. That village didn't do anything—Takhisis's servants did. Someone took advantage of that."

"Takhisis?" Cerisse asked, confused.

"The Dark Queen." Belen lowered her head in sorrow. "I learned about that during the time I was a dancer—the

War of the Lance was going on while I hid in Worver's circus. Takhisis and her evil dragons were breaking the peace between us all, stealing the eggs of the good dragons and using them—" her voice broke. Jace wanted to take her hand, but was afraid she wouldn't finish the story. After a moment, she continued. "Using them, twisted by magic, to make an army of draconians."

"I heard about that," Cerisse said. "They destroyed the good dragons' eggs. Is that what happened to your child? Oh, Belen, I'm so sorry."

Child? Jace hadn't reached that part of his thought process. The egg was Belen's child. He looked at her again, her long silver hair flowing down past her shoulders, beautiful, even features blurred with tears and grief. Belen was a mother?

"Belen . . . how old are you?" he asked, dumbfounded.

"If the dates on my letters are any indication," Belen answered quietly, "several hundreds of years."

That, Jace thought, was going to put a serious damper on any sort of dating.

"The person who convinced me to attack that village found out that my egg was missing—they may even have seen it stolen—and lied to me about who took it. I believed them." She let Ebano help her from the room. He half carried her to the wooden chair by the desk. She sat heavily, pulling the makeshift cloak tight around her shoulders. "They used me. They used my anger."

"Do you think the evil dragons did it?" Cerisse asked.

"I don't think so." Belen shook her head. "I would have recognized an evil dragon for what it truly was, no matter what spells hid its form. It was someone else."

"Can you remember anything at all? Who they were? What they said to you?"

Belen shook her head and met Jace's eyes frankly. "Only my anger. I remember that very well. There are memories, but they're very fragmented. I remember rushing down the stairs, into the courtyard, and then out over the forest with nothing on my mind except finding my egg. But I didn't find it." Her eyes teared up again, sparkling against frosted eyelashes. "It wasn't at the village."

She brushed back the tears, struggling to remember more of her past. "I don't know how I ended up wandering in the woods or how I found Worver's circus wagons instead of coming back to the tower."

"The stone's curse," Cerisse reminded her. "That's why you lost your memory."

With a sigh, Belen shook her head. "Dragons are difficult to enchant. Even if that stone was god-touched, I doubt it could have affected me if I didn't want it to. The stone may have taken my memory—but to do so, I must have given it up."

"You lost your egg, Belen, your child," Cerisse said evenly. "You had every right to be angry."

"But to attack an innocent village?" she protested. "How could I?" She stood up from the chair, the fur cloak falling askew around her. "I should have known."

Cerisse bristled. "You were asleep!" She shook her finger matter-of-factly in front of Belen's face. "I know that when I wake up, it takes me at least five minutes to figure out where I am, much less what I'm supposed to be doing that day. If someone ran into my wagon and woke me up yelling 'fire,' I'd be outside carrying buckets before I even asked where." She squared her jaw, fists on her hips. "You wrecked the village, but you didn't kill anyone. Mysos will have to recognize that."

"Why would he?" Jace groused. "He wasn't willing to give her the benefit of the doubt before, and even if we know what happened, we don't have any way to prove it."

"I deserve anything they do to me." Belen snatched up the fur again, her fingers sinking tightly into the white shag. "I attacked a village of innocents. I distracted them so that someone could steal the artifact they'd protected for generations. I'm as guilty as the person who took it.

I'll go back to Mysos and turn myself in. Whatever he and the White Robes of Palanthas want to do to me, I deserve it. I give up. I failed as a mother, and I failed to keep that village safe.

"I'm a *dragon*. I'm supposed to be better than that."

Before Jace had time to acknowledge how quickly Belen had grown accustomed to the idea of her true nature, Ebano stepped in. "Belen." The word was sharp, tinged with an unexpected anger. Everyone stopped what they were doing: Jace in his attempts to soothe her, Cerisse's indignant stomping. Even Belen paused, stopped by the hypnotist's pointed tone. "Foolish."

It was the sharpest tone Jace had ever heard from the genteel mystic. Ebano took the fur from her, folding it over his arm and laying it on the chair she'd just left. When he spoke again, his tone was back to its normal, smooth courtesy. "Your egg was you." He considered, and tried again. "Egg was . . . part of you. Family. This one understands what it is to lose family."

Pale sunlight trickled through the high window of the room, casting an unnatural pallor on the faces of the circus performers and bringing a deep mahogany glow to Ebano's face. He sighed, placing one hand on Belen's shoulder, and gave her a small smile. "This one's home far away. Desert sand. Very beautiful. Very dangerous." His smile faded.

"This one's family died. Wife. Very young daughter. This one wishes he had no memory. This one can only remember." He passed a hand over his pale purple eyes, closing them for a moment. When he opened them again, Jace could see great sorrow. "This one misses them, very much. Saw them everywhere, but they lived not. So this one ran."

Belen ran a hand through her silver hair, pushing it back from her face. "I didn't know about your family, Ebano."

The mystic shrugged. He took in a deep breath, pursing his lips. "This one was a coward."

"Ebano!" Cerisse broke in. "How can you say that? I saw you fight those werewolves. And if you could have reached the chimera, I know you would have fought it too. You're not a coward."

He brushed her words aside with a soft gesture. "Coward," he repeated. "Running away from memories. Homeland, house, everything. Memories." Ebano lowered his hand and fixed Belen with a somber stare. "Like you."

"Now, wait right there!" As always, Jace leaped to Belen's defense. He bristled at the mesmerist, his hands balling into fists. "Belen's no coward! That White Robe is hunting her! If anything, she's brave for wanting to turn herself in and face punishment for a crime that wasn't her fault!"

Cerisse looked torn.

"Coward." Ebano repeated without malice. "Running away, now run to prison. Prison still not here." He crossed his arms, hands sinking into the long sleeves of his dark purple robe. He stared meaningfully at Belen. "No memories there either. Safe."

"You take that back!" Jace felt heat rush into his face. Ebano was their friend! He'd come all this way, fought at their side, protected them—and now he called Belen a coward? The betrayal stung, making Jace's stomach clench. "Take it back, or I'll make you take it back." Without thinking, Jace's hand slid to his leg, dangerously near his sword hilt. Ebano didn't flinch. He simply met Jace's glare with a concerted smile.

Belen reached for Jace's elbow, pushing the boy back gently. "No, Jace. He's right."

"What?" Jace and Cerisse said together. Jace stared agape, but Cerisse protested.

"He doesn't know anything about you! You're a dragon, Belen, dragons aren't afraid of anything. How could he—"

Belen silenced Cerisse with a shake of her head. "He's absolutely right. If I let Mysos take me to Palanthas and put me in prison, even if I'm guilty, I never have to face this forest again. I never have to fix the mess I made in

Angvale, and I never have to see"—her voice caught, and she had to push to continue—"I never have to see that empty nursery again."

She straightened, looking up first at the sun on the frosted windowsills, then back to Jace, Cerisse, and finally Ebano. "I'd just be hiding."

"So what do we do?" Cerisse asked, tugging nervously at her auburn braid.

"I promised Mysos I would come back, and that's what I'm going to do. But I'm not going with him to Palanthas. I'm coming back here, whether he likes it or not, and I'm going to find out who is really responsible." She hugged Ebano impulsively, a bit of the circus dancer she'd been leaking through her radiant smile. "It's late. We'll stay here tonight, and then go back tomorrow morning. Mysos gave me three days. Once he hears what we've found, he'll have to give me more time. We can find whoever did this. We can put things back the way they were."

"When we do," Jace agreed with what he thought was an inspired flourish, "they'll pay for what they did to the villagers, and to you." Mother or not, Belen was still the most beautiful woman—dragon—he'd ever seen. Jace promised himself he'd never give up on trying to win her love.

Ebano, for his part, simply stared at Jace with those enigmatic purple eyes.

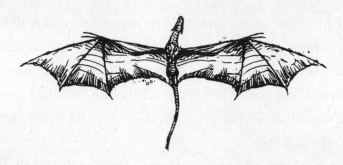

CHAPTER NINE

Belen's silver wings reflected the bright morning sunlight, shining like falling stars over the thick green forest. They'd left Belen's tower before the sun was fully in the sky, aware that the flight would take several hours. It was easier to go straight south than it had been to wander west in search of the tower. They knew where they were going, and the circus banners guided them as they came close. Eventually, those banners turned from bright spots on the horizon to fluttering pennants of silk, and Belen glided to the ground at the edge of the forest. "We'll walk from here," she said, transforming into her human guise, "so that the sight of a dragon doesn't frighten anyone."

"That's right," Cerisse chuckled. "The noon show! We'll get there right about the time everyone in the crowd is in their seats."

"We might even catch a bit of Hautos's barbell juggling." Belen smiled. "I can't wait to see Worver and tell him everything. He'll be so happy to know I didn't hurt those people." She beamed. Belen was much calmer this morning than she had been the day before. Having left behind the fears of the village and her anger at the tower, she walked down the path toward the circus with a light, determined step.

The last of the crowd was trailing in when the companions reached the outer ring of circus tents. Brilliantly colored pennants and banners fluttered in the strong wind. Street music filled the air, and the musicians' faces turned red as a clown's nose as they blew into their instruments. A few stragglers were still making their way into the big three-ring tent, dragging unruly children behind them.

The four friends passed the ticket-sellers with a friendly wave and a smile, passing beneath the gigantic, arched sign painted in reds and yellows that declared Worver's Amazing Celestial Circus of Light to be both incredible and mind-boggling. Cerisse bought them all popcorn. They hadn't eaten since they'd left the tower that morning, and Jace's stomach was churning from the salty smell of buttered corn and sweet caramel apples.

They slipped into the main tent, the sound of music jangling in their ears, and let themselves follow the crowd toward the seats. A performance was occurring in the central ring, highlighted by the blaze of three white spotlights.

"That's not Hautos," Jace said, eyes widening. "What is Worver doing?"

Down in the main ring, Worver had brought three large cages forward, each big enough to hold a horse. Inside these were man-sized wolves . . . no . . .

"Are those werewolves?" Cerisse spluttered, choking on some popcorn.

At a snap of Worver's whip and a quick tug on a silver chain held tightly in his other hand, the werewolf in the first cage roared and rose up onto its hind legs, swiping at the air. Worver guided it out of the cage by the chain, dragging the beast by a thick leather collar around its neck. With a few more snaps of the ringmaster's whip, the werewolf walked over to a stool and clambered upon it like one of Worver's trained lions.

"What is he doing?" Belen gasped. "Where did he get those werewolves?"

"Mantano," Ebano pointed, bursting in excitement. "Mantano!"

He was pointing at the locks and links of Worver's restraints. "Silver?" Jace asked. "Is that what 'mantano' means?"

Ebano nodded in glee, finally learning the word he'd wanted. "Yes! Silver!"

"That's what you use against werewolves? Wish we'd

known about that when they were attacking us," Cerisse groused. Jace elbowed her and she yelped. "What?"

"Those are *people*, Cerisse! Cursed and altered, but still humans who lived in the village of Angvale. They're not performance animals—they're slaves!"

Worver's voice boomed magically through the massive tent. "These amazing beasts are a remnant of royal wolf blood, once interbred with elves! Their twisted form— part elf, part wolf—is sign of their true nobility among the beasts of the forest. No predator can stand against them! No animal is their equal! You will see for your- selves in these few simple tricks that they have the form of an animal—but the intelligence of a man!" The crowd cheered wildly as Worver made the three werewolves do a few simple tricks—catching a ball and throwing it back, holding a hoop while another jumped through it, and counting to three when he showed them a row of brightly colored triangles.

"I hope one of them breaks out of that collar and bites him!" Jace snarled. "How could he do this?"

"He must not know. Worver would never enslave a person—he has to think they're just unusual animals. He probably had someone looking for us in the woods around Angvale," Belen guessed, "and found some of the wolves near the village. He might not even know what they are, other than magical beasts like the others he trains for the circus. We've got to get backstage and explain everything."

They crept backstage, pushing their way through crowds and sidling between rows of thrilled onlookers. The guards keeping audience members from the red curtains at the rear recognized them, greeting them in hushed whispers and quiet handshakes before pulling aside the velvet to let them slip past.

Worver's captured werewolves were rolled through shortly after, locked once again in their cages. The ringmaster followed behind them, rubbing his hands together in glee and chattering with the animal handlers. When his eyes fell on the companions, they opened as wide as platters, and he let out a joyful crow. "My dear, dear Belen! Jace! Cerisse and Ebano! You're back! And you're safe—thank goodness!" Worver clapped Ebano on the shoulder and reached to squeeze Cerisse's arm. "Did you find what you were looking for? Mysos—that horrible mage—has had his fingers in every single nook and cranny of this circus. He's nearly driven Hautos to drink, you know, with his poking about."

"No, Worver, actually—" Jace started.

"Worver," Belen said, "what are these creatures doing here? Don't you know they're dangerous?"

"My dear, my dear! Let's not forget what's truly

important—your well-being! Tell me, did you discover anything? Can we clear your name?" Before she could answer, Worver's little pet, the strange horned monkey, ran up his leg and perched on his shoulder with a chirping hiss. "Yes, yes, Tsusu, you're absolutely right. Perhaps we should have this conversation elsewhere, eh, my friends?" Worver winked, throwing his arm around Jace's shoulder. The beast snarled down at the boy, a thin line of drool connecting its upper fangs and lower jaw. "Come with me. We'll talk about it in one of the private wagons after these splendid beasts have been put away."

They followed Worver as he extolled the virtues of his new pets, with Jace struggling to get a word in edgewise. "Those beasts . . . " the boy tried again as they wound their way through the next set of performers and out into the open area behind the main tent. Jace, Cerisse, and Belen hurried along behind Worver, trying to keep up with the ringmaster's long, swift strides.

"Oh, yes! Exceptional, aren't they? Well, when you four didn't return after a whole day, I sent Hautos after you to make certain you were all right. The storm and all—we were terribly worried, you know. Trees fell down from the winds, and the rain nearly made the roof of the tent collapse, the water was so heavy. Trouble everywhere! And then you, not coming home to tell us you were all right, what was I supposed to think?" Worver shook his head. "While he was out there looking for you, Hautos found these amazing creatures! They can't be harmed. They are almost as intelligent as you or I—"

"Almost?" Belen bristled, but Worver didn't notice.

"They learn quickly and are able to replicate any trick I teach them. They're really quite amazing. They gave Hautos a bit of a rumble when he first captured them, tore into him quite fiercely, but the circus has ways of healing injured performers, you know that." Quickly, he shifted the subject, eager to excite them with his find. "It was Tsusu who used silver on them first while we were trying to get them into cages. Wonderful idea! Worked like a charm." Worver puffed up, smiling widely.

"Hautos was hurt?" Belen and Jace shared a glance. Jace went on, "Ringmaster, he might be in serious trouble! They might have . . . uh . . . "—he fumbled for some justification, suddenly uncomfortable telling the friendly ringmaster the whole truth—"diseases!"

"Oh, now, Jace my boy, don't you worry about that. I've got secret healing ways to keep this circus in running order, you know." Worver puffed out his chest and laid a finger beside his nose conspiratorially. "Didn't Francis the Firebreather turn out just fine even after that unfortunate oil spill? And when Ringo, the lion, had that accident with his claw—well that worked itself out quickly, you remember? No worries, my dear boy, have no worries at all!" Worver slapped Jace's shoulder, knocking the boy forward. "I love southern Solamnia! It seems every time I come to this area, something wonderful happens for the circus. First, Belen joined us—and you are staying, dear, aren't you? You've found a way? Ah, right, right, not here, we're almost to the wagon. Well, now, as for these magnificent beasts! Marvelous, just marvelous. They'll bring in a lot of good solid coin, I can tell you that."

"Ringmaster Worver!" Cerisse broke in. "You can't keep them!"

"What?" he paused in the main clearing between the circus wagons. "Of course I can! They're wild animals. No one owns them. Once we teach them a few more tricks, tame them a bit more, we can use them with the lions or let them perform on their own. You haven't had a chance to watch them really go through their tricks yet, but they're just—"

"People!" Belen cried out at last, clenching her fists. "They're people, Worver! You can't treat them like animals! They feel and they think, and they have rights!"

"Whatever are you talking about, poor girl?" Worver let go of Jace and reached to take Belen's hand. He patted it gently, roughing the skin of her wrist as if to wake her from a faint. "They're beasts! Splendid beasts." He leaned closer. "Money-making beasts!"

Jace's skin crawled. Worver had always been a bit money-hungry, but the way he talked about those poor, cursed werewolves was awful—even if they'd chased Jace and nearly killed him. Jace struggled with it for a few minutes, trying to justify Worver's point of view, but in the end he just couldn't keep quiet. "I agree with Belen. It's slavery to keep them. You have to let them go."

Worver patted his shoulder. "We'll discuss it later, dear boy. First, I want to hear everything that happened to you and my dear Belen."

Tsusu howled softly on the ringmaster's shoulder, running back and forth behind his head so quickly it jostled Worver's top hat. "Now, now." Worver let go of Belen and tried to soothe the beast. Turning to Jace and the others, the ringmaster said, "Let's go inside and settle all this. It's obvious that something's upset you. Difficult journeys can do that to you. We'll sit down and have a nice talk inside my wagon." Worver reached for Belen's elbow to encourage her along.

Belen pulled her arm out of the ringmaster's grip with a glare. "No. This is more important. Worver, aren't you listening? Those animals you have locked up, they're people under a curse, don't you see? That's what we found out." She grabbed his sleeve and forced him to stop.

"Are you sure, my dear? Perhaps you're mistaken." Worver looked flustered.

"We're very sure." Belen met his eyes squarely. "You have to let them go."

"I . . . I can't do that! We have shows planned, tickets that are already sold . . . "

"I can't work with a circus that keeps slaves, Worver." Belen was unshakable, and Jace felt tremendously proud. She'd never stood up to Worver before. Maybe this was a little bit of the dragon coming out? Whatever it was, Jace agreed with it.

"Me neither," Jace chimed in. Cerisse was quick to nod. Jaced looked around to see what Ebano thought.

Wait a minute. Where was Ebano?

"You can't possibly mean this, Belen! This is mutiny. After everything I've done for you?" Worver seemed genuinely hurt. He clasped one hand over his heart, his mustache trembling with woe.

"I do mean it. I have to, Worver. I learned a lot while we were gone, and I know who—and what—I am now. There are things I just can't allow to happen. I hope you understand." Her voice shook a little, and Jace could see what it took for her to stand up to the man who had saved her in the woods and given her a home.

"You really are the dragon?" Worver's voice fell, his

eyes wide. He looked at each of them, eyes questing for the truth.

"Yes," Belen said.

Worver turned back to Belen, considering. "And you're serious about leaving?"

"Yes." Belen lifted her head, her hair tossing about her shoulders. "And more, I'm going to free those werewolves and put them back in the forest whether you like it or not. I'm sorry, ringmaster, but you can't convince me that keeping them is anything but slavery."

"Well, I don't suppose I can convince you to change your mind, my dear, but I must say that you've put me in a very difficult spot. I simply can't let them go. I've already got too much money wrapped up in them, you see." He paused, sighed, and brushed his handkerchief across his forehead. "If you must go, I understand that, but please, at least allow me to offer you a place to stay the night and clean up. Here, there's a spare wagon right beside the animal cages. You can go in there, wash up, and I'll speak to Master Mysos and see if he'll meet with you tonight or in the morning. You must be simply exhausted. You're quite sure it's not just the weariness talking?"

"I'm sure, ringmaster," Belen said through tight lips. "I won't reconsider, and neither will my friends."

"Very well then," Worver sighed, guiding them to

a long red wagon with very thick beams holding up the flat ceiling. "Here, let me get the door." He held it open for them, letting them pass him by and climb the stairs into the wagon.

"A pity that it has to be this way, really," Jace heard Worver mumble grimly as the acrobat climbed past the ringmaster and up the stairs. "And I had such glorious plans."

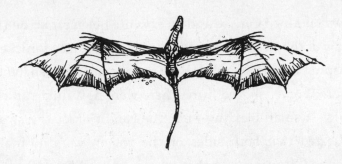

CHAPTER TEN

It was dark inside the wagon, and only the light of the open door shed any detail on the inside. Jace's first thought as he went through was that the ringmaster had put too much straw on the floor. He felt about in the darkness for any kind of chair or cot to sit on, cursing Cerisse's shadow that blocked the majority of the sunlight streaming in the bright doorway. It wasn't until the sunlight vanished behind them that he realized Worver had thrust Belen to the side, through another door, and clanged that shut before slamming the entryway.

Jace spun, nearly tripping over Cerisse, and realized that the inside of the wagon was lined with bars. "Worver!" he yelled, jerking on them in shock and frustration. "What are you doing?"

Now that his eyes had adjusted to the darkness, Jace could see that they'd been guided into one of the big animal wagons. There were two cages in this wagon—one now contained Cerisse and Jace, while Belen sat up on the straw of the other where she'd been shoved. Jace panicked, grasping for his sword only to realize it'd been snatched before Worver shoved him. There were no animals in the cages—a small blessing—but the condition of the straw indicated that both sides of the wagon were normally occupied. It was likely that whatever lived here was performing in one of the rings—and would return whenever Worver said so.

"Worver!" Jace yelled again.

"Terribly sorry, dear boy." Worver opened a slat in the rear of the cage, and Jace dived toward it. It was too small to slip through, but he wedged his hand in, hoping somehow to grab the ringmaster's throat and throttle him. Worver easily dodged, and instead stung Jace's hand with the little whip used to tame animals. "But there really is no other choice. A beastly pity! Your father was such an earner for the circus. I'd hoped you would be the same."

"What is this?" Cerisse wailed, scrabbling along the bars of the cage inside the wagon, looking for another way out. "What are you doing, Worver? I thought you were our friend!"

"He's going to kill us," Jace snarled, jerking his hand back and leaning close to the open slat. "Or, at least, he's going to try."

"Why?" Belen pounded on the wall. "Worver, you've always protected me, always helped me! What are you doing?"

Outside, Worver sighed. "I have no other choice. You've pushed me into a corner, and I must act in order to save my livelihood—my circus, you see—and if I don't, there are more than a few families that will be out of a job. Think of the Flying Wingates! Harwell, the clown family extraordinaire! The lions, the bears, the dancing dogs and their puppies—can you let them starve?"

Through the slat, Jace could see Worver placing a hand over his heart in mock sorrow. "Someone has to keep this circus going, and you were about to place a nail in our coffin."

"I can't believe it." Belen sank to her knees, covering her face with her hands. "I trusted you!"

"I cared for you, my dear girl, like a daughter! But I cannot allow you to return those werewolves—nor, in fact, can I allow you to leave the circus." His voice fell to a dark hiss. "Ever."

Jace felt his stomach sink. "Worver, you can't get away with this. People will notice!"

"Who will notice? Did you speak to anyone before you left the tent with me?" Worver laughed.

Jace admitted to himself that he had not, and the

realization dried his throat, making it feel as if it were filled with ash.

Worver continued, "Hautos found those wonderful beasts—he was following your trail when he came across them in the forest. Luckily for us all, Hautos relishes a good fight. He managed to to catch a few and bring them here for the show. They're better off in the circus, you see? We'll take care of them, ensure they're fed, and keep them from any harm."

"Worver!" Belen burst out, shocked. "You can't do that! Those are people!"

"So you say, but they're not people right now. They're revenue, dear Belen. And now that you have betrayed me, so are you." Worver frowned, steepling his hands around a trinket that hung from a chain around his neck. He twirled it back and forth, rolling it between the pads of his fingers thoughtfully. "I'd make this easier on us all, my dear, but I'm afraid you're a dragon. You're immune to my usual tricks—blackmail, threats, mesmerism, the standard things I use to keep all the acts working under my big top. I'm forced to use something more vulgar—like your friends.

"'I don't enjoy this, my dear, I hope you understand that. I'm not the kind of man who would abuse a delicate jewel such as yourself, but you've pushed me to the limit!

My entire circus is at stake, and quite frankly, that means more to me than your good humor."

"You're horrible!" Belen burst out.

"Tut-tut, my dear! Come, I'm asking you again to change your mind. Just think of the money we'll make! Can you imagine how famous we'll be with you in our midst? Worver's Amazing Celestial Circus of Light—now, with a real dragon! People will ride for miles in every direction just to attend the shows. Children will plead to return again and again. Ticket sales will go through the roof, and still, people will pay hard-earned steel just to catch a glimpse of you! I tell you what, Belen. I'll give you, hmm, three percent of the entire take per season. What do you say?"

She clenched her fists and spat back at him, "Never!"

Cerisse's jaw hung open, and she and Jace shared a look of horror. They'd known Worver was a greedy man, but they'd never suspected the lengths he'd go to just to make a profit. Unfortunately, now that they knew, they were in serious trouble.

"I won't do it," Belen said through gritted teeth. "I'm not a circus animal!"

"You're a performer, Belen. You were when you danced in the big top, and you were just as much one when you came in from the woods, weeping and moaning and claiming you didn't remember anything. A magnificent performance, my dear, a sign of true quality. At the end of these last five years, even I was beginning to believe you. You have a sincere dedication to the bit, and I commend you for your fortitude!" Worver chuckled deep in his throat. "I'll speak to Mysos about it, convince him that the best punishment for you is to stay right where you are. We might have to call it a charity function—give a little bit to the people of the area, so on, so forth, but still! Extremely lucrative, I'm sure you'll see. Best of all, if you refuse, I can convince the White Robes of Palanthas to swoop in and take you away."

Jace shuddered at the sight of Worver's toothy, mustached smile beyond the thin opening in the wagon slats. He wasn't sure if the ringmaster would go through with his threats, but at this point, Jace wasn't sure of anything that had to do with Worver. The ringmaster twisted his hands together as if he were already counting the coins.

"We will earn glorious amounts of money! Hand over fist!" Worver chuckled. "In time, you'll be glad I did this, Belen. If not for me, this circus would have failed a hundred times. Our headliner, Jordan the Undaunted, was gone! No one will come to see a circus without a headliner." Worver twisted his mustache. "In any case, I must bid you farewell. The trapeze act is about to end, and they need me to introduce the contortionists."

"Wait, what about us? Are you just going to leave us here?" Cerisse pounded on the wall of the wagon.

"Oh, goodness no." The ringmaster chucked. "I'm going to kill you. I do regret it. It's a terrible pity that Belen won't agree to my terms. Jace will never redeem his family name, and Cerisse, I really will miss your exceptional act. When you juggle those little flaming rods—magnificent! I don't expect to replace you quickly, that's a certainty."

"What's to stop me from just turning into a dragon and tearing out your throat?" Belen bristled.

Worver smiled at her through the thin opening. "If you change form now, Belen, you'll crush this entire wagon—and make your friends little more than stains against those bars." His smile faded, and his dark eyes were sad. "I'm afraid I must, my dear. Killing them is for the best. Not only will it convince you that I'm serious, but it will also prevent anyone from telling the White Robes what's gone on. By the time this is over, I'll have a writ from the White Robes to keep you here under my control, and if you should break that writ or attack me . . . well, I think that being hunted down by the White Robes of Palanthas and destroyed should be deterrent enough."

"I'll tell them what you've done, Worver, I swear it!" Belen screamed in anger.

"Go ahead, my dear. No one is going to believe a

murderous dragon who's lost her memory. This is probably just another episode, you see." He sighed and looked up at the sun to gauge the time. "Now, I'm afraid I really must go. Farewell, all. Belen, I'll see you when you're feeling a bit more reasonable." The sliding window snapped shut, and Jace heard a latch being thrown on the far side of the wall.

Jace heard the back of the wagon slide open. Beyond was another cage, one of the mobile ones, now locked against the wagon's side. Jace could see Hautos levering the front panel of iron bars aside so that the monster could enter the traveling wagon safely.

And what a beast it was! Clicking its horrible crab claws together, the creature scuttled forward into the wagon on thin, clawlike legs that were serrated like dagger blades. Thick, chitinous armor, like the carapace of a lobster, covered its upper body.

"Arcox," Cerisse choked, backpedaling. "That's the arcox!"

With a snort of laughter, Hautos slammed the wagon bars shut once more, lowering the side of the wagon swiftly to seal them inside the dim cage area. Jace could see the bars through the other cage, past the arcox where the mobile cage's bars were open rather than wood. Worver waved his high black hat at them. "Good-bye, dear friends," Worver bellowed. "Belen, we'll discuss the terms of your first performance after I speak with Mysos. I'm certain he'll be very understanding." From Worver's smile, the ringmaster was certain that his victory was just a matter of time. Tsusu, his horrible monkeylike pet, did a flip on Worver's shoulder as the arcox stepped in and the big wooden door of the wagon slid closed between the mobile cage and the creature's rear. Outside, Jace heard the sound of locks being shot all around the wagon.

"Cerisse!" He backed up, keeping an eye on the gigantic monster at the far end of the wagon. "Do you have any weapons?"

"I set my backpack down in the big top. I didn't think I'd need it!"

He gulped. "Don't you keep spare daggers on your belt? For practice?"

"Well, uh, let me see what's in my pockets. I've got an apple, three darts . . . a couple of candles, and some pocket lint. You?"

"Not even that much." They took a few more steps back as the monster turned to face them, clicking its horrible claws in eager anticipation of a meal. Belen gripped the bars of her cell, shaking them and calling to the creature. For a moment, it turned toward her, snapping claws on the bars, but it was unable to reach through them to hurt her.

Bored with prey it couldn't attack, the arcox moved back toward Jace and Cerisse.

Jace scanned the bars, hoping to climb them, but saw no handholds. Even if he were pressed against the ceiling, the arcox's long claws could probably reach him. Frustrated, he moaned, "This is it. We're done for. Worver wins."

"Wait a second," Cerisse blurted out. "Where's Ebano?"

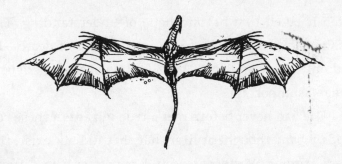

CHAPTER ELEVEN

*M*y name is Ebano Bakr Sayf al-Din ibn Ceham, prince of *Sayf, a people who once belonged to the tribe known as Khur. Now, the Sayf are dead, buried in the deep deserts of our homeland. I have traveled many lands and seen many wonders, praise Keja who united us, and curse his seven sons. The truth has been revealed to me, my family taken from me, and I have nothing left in this world except the fire of life and the water of forgiveness. Thus I move in honesty. Thus I act with integrity. Thus I kill without malice. Hear my sole prayer, noble gods: grant me an honorable death. Alak-al-saham-din-al-bhar, may the blessings of the gods be upon the world.*

Ebano folded his arms together, watching as the ringmaster led the others away toward the wagons. Their slow language sounded of drool and slick stones, and too often it bored him beyond hope of understanding. This was not important. The mage in the robes of death—he, and only he—could free the lady dragon from her curse. That was important.

He had never before met a true wizard in these cold lands. Ebano thought at first that they did not exist, that these strange Westerners could not grasp the difficult arcane studies needed to master the powers of the arcane. Then this "Palanthas wizard" arrived, dressed all in white. He looked like a mourner at a funeral, forbidden to wear color or go out for seventy days—ten days for each of Keja's gods-cursed sons, as tradition dictated.

Then he had seen the man in white robes, and at last, Ebano understood. To become a wizard here was to commit oneself to death alone. No wonder the crowds stared at Ebano for even the simplest of tricks. They assumed that he, too, was death-touched like their own spell-casters.

I must find him, and I must face him, Ebano thought. He made the sign of blessing before his eyes. One of the contortionists waved back at him, and Ebano smiled. As usual, these primitives did not understand. No matter. The gods would judge them, heretics and heathens alike.

Ebano's eyes narrowed as he strode through the narrow causeways, ignoring the roar of the crowd seeping through the thick canvas of the big top. I will face him, this western wizard who threatens the dragon girl, and I will make him undo what he has done.

The fluttering canvas of the big tent drew his mind back to other days. He remembered raw sand beneath his crunching boots, the whinny and storm of horses, ready to race against the sandstorms of the desert and win. These things, simple memories, came back to him when he least deserved their comfort but most needed it. Blessing the hand of Keja and the gods, Ebano paused to bow and touch his forehead, lips, and heart in supplication. If his family's souls were with him, then he could not fail, no matter if he lived or died.

It was easy to find the wizard, even in this sea of tents haphazardly thrown together. They looked like desert flotsam at a stagnant oasis. The ringmaster was a man consumed with the sin of Hachakee, Keja's fourth son, who bore the curse of pride. Worver would keep the death wizard close. *There.* Beside the ringmaster's magnificently painted wagon stood another, smaller and less ornate. Worver was forcing the wizard into small quarters, cramped and uncolored, to humble him. Ebano felt his lip curl. These people know no end of insults to their betters, he thought. This death wizard must be strong indeed to accept such affronts. Challenging him will be honorable. I hope he dies well, or kills me with swiftness.

Ebano knocked upon the door of the wizard's dwelling, amused as always at the strange custom of rapping one's knuckles on stiff, heavy wood. Someone inside gave a customary greeting, one which Ebano recognized needed no reply. Was he to go inside, then? The mesmerist closed his eyes, praying to Keja for patience, and knocked again.

This time, the death wizard pulled the door open and faced him, white funeral robes swirling in the wake of the heavy wooden door. He stared at Ebano as if expecting a message. Of course, Ebano thought. He does not know who I am, or how to respect me, because I do not wear the deathly white robes. I must educate him. A small thing to do for an honorable opponent.

"May the peace of Keja, blessed is his name, be upon you." Ebano bowed, once more making the gesture of blessing—forehead, lips, and heart. The traditional words of challenge in his native tongue came to him easily, even after so many years. "I am Ebano Bakr Sayf al-Din ibn Ceham, prince of Sayf, master of the arcane arts, and I challenge you to a formal duel. My honor has been tarnished, and your blood must wash it clean."

The death wizard said something incomprehensible, furrowing his brow. Alas, the man did not know a civilized tongue. Ebano tried again, using the simple words in their language that he had been taught, to better communicate with these foreigners. "This one is Ebano," he said, using their awful-sounding language. "Fight." There. That should be straightforward enough.

"Fight?" The walker of death tried to look behind Ebano, searching for something that was not there. Ebano was not fooled.

"Fight." He considered, and then remembered one of the formal phrases that the ringmaster had taught him to impress the crowd. He babbled it carefully, remembering the syllables by heart without knowing their meaning. He was moderately sure that one could be a threat, as most of the people who heard it during his act would stare at him afterwards, wide-eyed and pale faced.

The death wizard only looked more confused. He said something in his thick tongue, but the only words that Ebano caught were "Worver," "time," and "dragon."

Dragon! Yes, the dragon, Ebano nodded enthusiastically. This all comes down to her, he thought. My honor, my shameful past, the deaths of my family—here and now, I can redeem them all!

He readied himself for the first rush of magic, the flow of adrenalin and combat, but the death wizard pushed right past him and out into the courtyard, where he stood with his hands on his hips, looking around. He turned back to Ebano and gestured impatiently.

Idiot. Ebano ground his teeth in frustration. This time, the death wizard would not mistake Ebano's meaning. The prince of Sayf strode out to meet him, scooped up a handful of dust, and blew it straight into the bearded mage's face.

So, too, will you become dust.

May the peace of Keja be upon both of our souls.

He followed that up with a punch, knocking the white-garbed wizard backward.

While the other wizard was spluttering to regain his footing, Ebano began to summon the power of his art. *Dark and fell tide, rise at my call! I summon the spirit of Fin-Maskar, the seventh son of Keja, whose sin was wrath.*

Fire exploded around Ebano's hand, lighting the dark-skinned mesmerist in flickering splendor. His enemy's eyes widened, and Mysos managed to chant a few words that quickly raised a shield of energy between them as Ebano's flame roared down. The shield held, and fire licked out all along the ground, spilling over the sides, ripping in a hiss through the air from Ebano's raised hand.

The instant that the fire stopped, the death mage was ready with retaliation. Bolts of energy flew forth from his outspread fingers as the shield moved aside. They uncoiled in arcing white stripes of light, launched directly toward Ebano's purple eyes. Before they could strike him, Ebano waved his hand, clearing the air of energy as if he were swatting flies. Each of the wizard's bolts struck lightly against Ebano's fingers. They hissed like hot irons plunged into snow and vanished.

Facing his opponent with more respect, the man in mourning robes squared off and studied Ebano. He said something in their thick language that sounded aggressive, and Ebano smiled. "Let action, not words, dictate our understanding." Never before had the words of Keja felt so appropriate, even if the wizard in white robes made a confused squawk in response. Ebano began the spell again, gathering energy like the reins of a desert horse, feeling it slip through his fingers as he wove and tugged, drawing each thread into a cloak of power. With a spin, Ebano released it, watching it coalesce into silvery mist that hurtled through the air to a spot just above the other wizard's head. It exploded like fireworks, sending a shower of sparks raining through the air.

The mage rolled, getting dust all over his white robes, but he was too slow. Wherever the sparks touched— his clothing, the grass—stone grew like a crust. Struggling against the enchantment, the other man coiled his magic, lashing out at the charm again and again until the stone began to shatter. Despite Ebano's hope that it would overcome the wizard, he broke free, slapping his hand against the ground in a violent display. The earth broke open and a crack raced toward Ebano, forcing him to use his levitation trick to jump away before he was consumed by the earth.

By now, they'd drawn a crowd. Several of the performers had spilled out the back of the big top, staring in shock and awe at the open displays of sorcery erupting in the rear clearing. Two of the trapeze artists huddled in one another's arms, squealing as sparks from Ebano's spell blew too near. The mesmerist straightened his shoulders, throwing his head high. Fear or admiration? It did not matter. In this moment, he was once again a prince defending his honor, protecting his people from their enemies. This was the purpose Keja had given to his life, the purpose he had lost, when—

"Mysos!" one of the bystanders screamed in fear. Yes, that was the name of the western wizard in his white mourning robes. The ringmaster had said it in his wagon before they left, when they were pleading with the wizard for Belen's life—the same way that his wife had pleaded for their daughter's.

Ebano twitched aside, letting a bolt of crackling, arcing electricity course past him to strike the ringmaster's wagon. There was a snapping of wood and a terrible smell of ozone, and when the smoke cleared, a black, charred scar ran all along the wagon's brightly painted side. He smiled serenely. The wizards here were far less talented than those he served with when he fought under Salah-Khan, when the Khur tribe sought to unify with the rest of those in the deep deserts.

"You face Ebano Bakr Sayf al-Din ibn Ceham! It was I who carried the banner of my tribe. I who led the charge of my people's mounts into battle, I who defeated and conquered others in the name of Khurdish unity! You cannot stand against me, dealer of death!" Sadly, it was obvious that the Westerner had no understanding of the boast. The man reached to draw some other spell material from his belt and stared at Ebano most absurdly. Ridiculous primitives!

Ebano tried again, stiffening and raising his hand with a flourish. "Hear me, you pale and unsightly blemish on the face of the gods' land! You face a true mage! I have fought beneath the claws of a dragon! I feared him not, and I do not fear you!"

The crowd made squawks of fear and anticipation. Perhaps one among them had enough command of civilized languages to recognize the wonders and marvels of a good boast in combat—or perhaps they were simply impressed by the magic flying about in the clearing. Whatever it was that made their eyes widen, Ebano welcomed it. This, indeed, would be a good place to die.

"Daddy!"

The cry came from one of the children clustered in the rapidly growing audience, the circus visitors unsure if this was part of the show. The cry turned Ebano's head instinctively, and an old memory flashed before his eyes.

Mysos spun, his white robes swirling out like the mad dances performed by dervishes in the deep desert, his hands snapping out, thrusting a ball of dark, crackling energy toward Ebano. It tracked his movement, making it impossible for him to dodge it or knock it aside. He would have to face the magic directly and control it before it could detonate.

Without flinching, Ebano stretched out his hands and caught the whirling ball of darkness. He spun it though his own magical control, swirling it around and around between his hands. It was no mean feat, and Ebano could feel sweat breaking out on his forehead as he shifted and spun the magic, twisting it into a tighter ball, refusing to allow it to untangle. Mysos stared at him openly, trying to concentrate on the spell and regain control, but Ebano was too strong. Their wills clashed, pushing against one another, fighting for supremacy, until at last Ebano gained enough ground to hurl the ball of darkness into the broken crevice at his feet. It plunged downward several feet, unraveling as it did. Ebano lunged aside, desperate to get out of the way before the magic was fully activated.

That was when he saw the crying child escape his mother's arms. A pale-haired little boy, blue eyes terrified and panicked, fled across the crowd and into the clearing. Without thinking, he stumbled too close to the crack as it shattered and broke apart.

In his mind's eye, Ebano saw not only the fight before him, but also one that happened long years ago.

I see a green dragon swooping in the sky, carrying the warlord Salah-Khan. The tribe of Sayf had fought bravely in the warlord's service, but scattered as his wrath turned upon them for their failure. The terrible greenish mist began to fall from the sky in a horrible smoking rain. Men fell, choking. Horses, the pride of his tribe, screamed in agony as their lungs filled with acid gas. My wife. My daughter—

Instead of counterattacking or escaping from the white robed wizard, Ebano spun. He whirled, twisting back toward the child. He reached out, hands grasping the child's tunic. He dragged the child close, tucking the screaming boy against his chest as he turned away from the earth's collapse. The spell finally collapsed, erupting from the deep earth with a whooshing hiss of foul, stinking acid. A fountain punched up through the crevice, exploding with thick goo, horrible searing smoke, and hissing poison. Had it struck Ebano in the chest, the blast would have consumed him. As it was, the crevice was too narrow, too shallow to hold it all—and it escaped into the clearing with a massive, spewing explosion. Ebano felt the acid burn into his back, sear through his dark robes, and burn away flesh and velvet alike. A wash of it flowed over him, droplets spurting through the air all around. All he could do was hold the child close and pray.

Memories flooded him.

The dragon has her in its claws, and my fingers are sliding from her dress. Amani! If only I had remained loyal to Salah-Khan, he would not have avenged himself on us. If I had seen through his false smiles, kept our tribe away from his dark purposes, if I had listened to you when you whispered in the bedchamber that he was an evil man. But I did not, and we followed him to our doom.

It was our love that destroyed us. I told Salah-Khan that you had spoken against him, that my own wife dreaded his cause and mistrusted his purpose. I remember how Salah's eyes flashed when I said it, how he did nothing that eve, but stayed silent as the grave. Only after he had sent my tribe out to conquer did he act. When we returned, my wife was dead, murdered by his guard's hands, condemned as a dishonorable, faithless traitor to the Khan.

That was the moment when I knew she had been right.

The Sayf fought. We fought against the Khan, the Khur that had been our brothers, and against his dragon, the mighty Green named Chokingdeath. Many of my men, my comrades, my brothers, died with my name on their lips. Some choked in the gaseous breath of the monster, spending their last strength to render mercy to suffocating, unconquerable steeds before our warriors fell across their saddles on the desert sand.

I, alone, survived.

My daughter, my Amani, was lifted by the claws of the Khan's massive green serpent. Ripped from my very hands, her dress sliding through my fingers as she was lifted into the heaven, Chokingdeath's final retribution for our revolt. The dragon's claws were wrapped about her. For my failure to protect Amani—to protect all of them—I am doomed to walk the earth until Keja finally grants me peace and lets me rest once more in my dead wife's arms.

He opened his eyes and saw the real world around him, shockingly hard and painful and real. The acid on his skin burned, scorching deep to the bone of Ebano's back. The child in his arms writhed and screamed, slipping out between arms too weak to hold him as Ebano fell forward onto the dusty ground. Unharmed, he fled back to his mother and buried himself in her skirts.

Ebano lay still upon the ground, hearing nothing but the pulse of his heart. The smell of poison-charred flesh, the same smell that had risen when the dragon breathed upon his men, filled his nostrils along with the heavy scent of dust and sweat. He had tried, tried to be a loyal general and prince, tried to save his daughter, tried to rescue Belen from the curse that had so clearly been laid upon her. The foreign wizard approached, stood over him, said something incomprehensible, and then turned away.

As the hem of the death wizard's white mourning robe filled Ebano's vision, he choked back an agonized laugh. The Westerner did not even have the courage to send Ebano fully to his death, denying him in the end both victory and salvation. I must die in battle, Ebano thought, or I will be kept from grace. He tried to push himself up to claw at the wizard's robe, but it twitched away from his fingers before Ebano could muster even a single clawing scratch.

Keja help me, he thought, clenching his fingers in agony and falling back against the dust. And may the gods remember that I tried.

In the end, that was all any man could do.

My name is Ebano Bakr Sayf al-Din ibn Ceham, prince of Sayf, a tribe and a land now buried in dry sand, swallowed by the *deep deserts of Khur. The truth has been revealed to me, my family taken from me, and I have nothing left in this world except the fire of life and the water of forgiveness. Alak-al-saham-din-al-bhar, may the blessings of the gods be upon the world.*

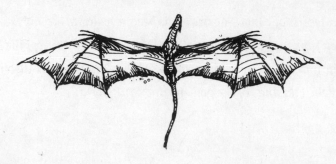

CHAPTER TWELVE

The arcox snapped its crablike claws, slicing them through the air in an eager rhythm as it scuttled toward the friends. Jace dodged left. Cerisse leaped to the right, dividing its attention. One thing they'd learned in the short amount of time they'd been in a cage with the beast was that the arcox wasn't very smart. This time, it followed Jace as he danced around the edge of the cage against the wagon's internal bars. Cerisse jumped up, pulling herself almost flat against the bars of the ceiling. It wouldn't protect her from the arcox's reach, but it kept the monster's attention on Jace while she rested for a moment. Soon, she would do the same for Jace.

They'd done this trick twice before, and this time, the beast was wary. It paused in its flight after the nimble boy, eyestalks turning back to look for the girl. "It's on to us!" Jace yelled, waving his hands back and forth. The arcox wasn't buying it. It turned on four pointed rear claws and charged for Cerisse, clicking its lobster claws over its head to reach for her. Cerisse dropped instantly, but cried out as her ankle twisted in the hay. She collapsed, and Jace couldn't see her anymore over the chitinous armored back of the arcox. "Cerisse!"

Belen was closer, although the bars of her cage kept her from reaching out or directly intervening. She stopped pounding on the wall of the wagon and turned quickly toward them. She hurled a hard lump of earth from the floor of the wagon and struck the arcox in one of its delicate eyestalks. The monster screeched and slowed, but did not change its course of attack. It had already learned that Belen was out of reach. Still, the pause gave Cerisse the opportunity to get to her feet. She stood unevenly, gingerly putting weight on the ankle, and shook her head dismally at Jace.

With two of her three darts—the only weapons they had in the wagon—in her hands, Cerisse faced the horse-sized arcox, dodging beneath the first sweep of its mighty claws. It was a waste of time to counterattack the crablike pincers, as they were thickly armored. The only place that the armor didn't cover was the beast's underside. It showed only when the arcox reared up to attack.

Like it was doing now.

Cerisse dived forward—exactly the opposite of what

the monster expected—and threw herself under the arcox. She slid between its six thin, pointed legs, kicking herself farther beneath them until they surrounded her like a sapling forest. Holding the darts tightly, she thrust upward, burying the long points into the arcox's belly. The monster let out a thin shriek, first trying to pedal backward, then when it bumped into the bars of the cage, sprinting forward to escape the pain. It left Cerisse lying on her back and ran directly toward Jace.

Claws outstretched, blood dripping from shallow wounds on its stomach, the arcox snapped at him, forcing him to dance between its claws. One caught his shoulder, snipping through the cloth and skin in an instant. It wasn't a direct hit or it might have removed Jace's arm, but as it was, white bone showed where the claw withdrew. Jace let out a muffled yell of pain and quickly spun away.

"Jace!" Belen yelled. "Are you— "

"I'll live! Can you pull it off me?"

"I can try." Unable to walk swiftly, Cerisse bit down on the remaining dart, jumped up, and grasped the bars of the ceiling. Agile as ever, she swung forward, flipping from hand to hand toward him faster than many people could run. She threw herself onto the back of the arcox and wrapped her legs tightly around its wide, armored back.

"Hooo!" she yelled between gritted teeth, wrapping her hands around the arcox's head.

The beast shrilled again, lifting its claws to snap them. Cerisse pressed herself flat against the armored back, causing the pincers to flail a few inches above her flapping auburn braid. "We need to do something about this!" she cried out. "We can't keep it busy forever!"

"Yeah," Jace gasped, ripping a sleeve from his shirt and tying it around his wound. "I noticed!"

"I have to do something!" Belen struggled with the thought, jerking helplessly at the thick iron bars that separated them. "I'm a dragon!"

"If you change form, we all get crushed against the bars. You're too big. You'll smash the wagon!" Jace shot her a comforting look. "We'll handle it!"

Belen growled, tearing at the bars in a frenzy, her gray eyes burning with a bright anger. Jace knew he didn't have much time before Belen sank into another one of her fugues, as she'd done at the tower. She might forget their situation entirely and attack, changing into the mighty dragon without understanding where she was or what she was doing, and if she did that, he and Cerisse would surely die.

"Can you get the point of the dart under its armor from back there?" he called, dashing around the wagon.

The arcox had noticed him again. Since it couldn't reach Cerisse or Belen, he'd become the target of its rage.

"Trying!" the half-elf yelled, tossing about on the arcox's plated back. "Tip's too short, and my hand's weak from the chimera's poison. I can't thrust hard enough! Curse it, these darts were designed for juggling or throwing at corkboard, not for killing a gigantic lobster! We need another weapon!"

Belen backed away from the bars and was stared at her hands. "Jace, am I a woman who turns into a dragon, or am I a dragon that turns into a woman?" she asked suddenly.

He blinked. "What?"

"Answer the question!" she screamed at him, eyes glinting with a strange intensity. Her skin had turned grayer, her body seemed larger than the slight form of the dancer he remembered. Was she losing herself again?

"Belen, calm down!" he yelled. "You've got to calm—"

Cerisse shrieked over him, breaking into his sentence, "Dragon, Belen! You're a dragon! You're only a person because you *want* to be! Now somebody help me with this thing—I only have one dart left!"

"Then if the spell breaks," Belen spoke in measured tones, her breathing tight and controlled, "I turn into a dragon." She stared down at her hands, where small scales glistened like a silk sheath over her skin.

"Yes, right. Exactly!" Jace ducked under the arcox's claws once more and heard them clang against the iron bars behind where he'd been standing, but found himself in the corner of the cage with nowhere to go. The monster lunged, Cerisse still clinging to its back. She lifted a fist and punched it atop its armored head, and it stumbled, missing him by only a few inches. In the space between sharp claw clacks, Jace managed to squeak between its chitinous body and the bars. The arcox must have felt him there, because it shuffled sideways to trap him.

The monster was heavy. Jace found himself edged between the thick plates of the arcox's shell and the heavy iron bars of the cage. The monster rammed sideways, scuttling on thin legs, and the force of the blow knocked all the air out of Jace's lungs. He choked, scratching and kicking at the arcox to try to knock one of the spindly legs out from beneath the monster, but nothing was working. The creature only pressed harder, refusing to budge even when Cerisse kicked and punched at it from above. It was going to crush him to death!

"So if something that is a part of me becomes no longer a part of me, then it's dragon. Not human." Belen wasn't making any sense—or maybe it was the shooting stars that Jace saw exploding in his vision that kept him from understanding her. She froze for a moment longer, and then jerked her hands apart. Jace glimpsed blood on her palm, and her face drained of color. "Cerisse!" she cried. "Catch!"

Something silvery and bright spun through the air, whisking between the bars. Instinctively, the juggler reached up to catch it, her certain hands grasping it tightly. She arched back on the arcox's shoulders and then plunged it downward, shouting her anger and her fear with a wild cry. The purple bandage fluttered around her wrist, her eyes as wild as a deep-forest elf as she attacked the beast. The shining blade in her hand looked like some sort of a dagger twinkling between her fingers. Where had Belen found that? It sank between the gap of the arcox's thick plating like water through a sieve.

The monster screamed, and it was the first real sound of pain they'd heard from it since being locked in this cage. It writhed, crushing Jace further. Cerisse scrambled on its back, drawing the blade out to stab again. The arcox broke away from the bars and charged across the cage, hurtling toward the far side of the cage at breakneck speed. Cerisse hung on tight, bringing the dagger down a third time even as the arcox threw itself against the wagon wall. It hit so hard that Cerisse was thrown free. She tumbled to the ground in front of the monster, the shining silvery blade still clutched in her hand. The bars creaked, and the wood above them began to splinter. The wagon's roof shuddered, and Belen let out a little cry.

"Cerisse!" Jace screamed, falling to his knees. It felt like his ribs were broken, and he could hardly draw a breath.

She didn't stop fighting, twisting to her feet like a cat. One of the arcox's claws caught her on a backswing, the thick curve of its closed pincer cracking against her injured arm. Cerisse let out a scream of pain but leaped in the air to avoid the sharp blade of its clacking claw. She landed between its writhing pincers and threw herself forward again, toward the monster's eyes. It dodged to avoid her, backing into the bars

A quick slash, and she cut through one stalk, then another, and the arcox was blinded. Cerisse dodged the vicious pincers once more and plunged the dagger forward, cutting between the chest plates of the arcox with a vicious swipe.

The creature stumbled, tottered, and fell. Cerisse crumpled to her knees in front of it, gasping for breath. Jace made his way toward her, picking through the hay and crawling over the arcox's fallen form. He reached out and touched her shoulder. "Cerisse, are you all right?"

Belen was already on the other side of the bars,

tugging where the arcox had caused the wood of the roof to splinter. While Jace helped Cerisse slowly to her feet, Belen managed to separate the bars enough to squeeze through. "I think the weight on the bars broke part of the roof," she called out, standing on her tiptoes to pound a board loose. "We might be able to climb through and get outside." Even at this distance. Jace could see that Belen's left hand was bloodied, her fingertips leaving slick red traces on the wood.

He looked down at the dagger still clutched in Cerisse's hand and untwisted her fingers from the base of the blade. It wasn't a dagger. There was no hilt, no real blade, only a thickly curved shaft, pointed at one end with a razor-sharp edge and a stubby, bloody base. "This is a claw." He stepped back, surprised.

"I did what I had to do." Belen didn't look down, climbing up the bars awkwardly to pound against another loose board. He saw her wince with each motion, one hand twisted in her shirt. Blood stained the fabric, seeping from a hidden wound. "I'm a dragon, changed by magic. So anything that's part of me that is separated from me changes back. That's how magic works."

"What did you do?" He stared at her.

Slowly, Belen pulled her hand out of her shirt, letting the folds of fabric unwind. He could see the injury now.

The nail of her first finger had been ripped away, leaving a bloody wound. He stared aghast.

"You tore your fingernail out?"

She ignored him. "Help me get these boards down, and we can climb out of here."

"Climb out?" Jace was near panic. "First we get attacked by a chimera, then the arcox. Cerisse is still sick from poison, and that arcox nearly cut my arm off, not to mention the fact that I think I have a couple of broken ribs. Now you want us to climb out of here . . . and do what? Fight Mysos? Stop Worver? We don't even know where Ebano went. For all we know, he was working for the ringmaster!" The sight of her wound struck him more deeply than the pain in his side or the injury that Cerisse suffered fighting the chimera. The idea that she'd hurt herself, willingly . . . that wasn't heroic at all.

"What?" Cerisse quirked an eyebrow.

"Oh, Jace." Sighing sympathetically, Belen shook her head. "You've been looking at this whole adventure as if it were just another performance. If we did well enough, it'd all turn out right in the end. The audience would applaud, the curtain would go down, and there'd be an encore."

He nodded. "In the end, we'd go home, take off the makeup, change out of our costumes, and everything would be great again, just like it was before. But we can't do that, can we? Things can't go back to the way they were." Jace didn't want to look at Belen or see that strange pity in her eyes.

"No, Jace." Now it was Cerisse's turn to pull him to his feet. "We can't. Not everything's a stage show. The world isn't like a magician with only one trick. Pull the rabbit out of the hat, and once it's out—where are you? The curtain closes, and when it opens tomorrow, the rabbit will be back in the hat? It doesn't work that way, things endlessly repeating over and over. Everything changes."

"She's right." Belen's lips curled into a slow smile. "That's how magic—that's how *life*—works." She reached out to them, grasping both of their hands between hers. "What are you afraid of, Jace?"

Losing you. He wanted to say it, meant to say it, but the words wouldn't come out. Everything up to now had been such a grand adventure, a chance to show Belen that he would fight for her, that he could be counted on, trusted. He hadn't even thought about what it might cost until he'd seen what Belen had done to herself in order to save them. "I thought we were heroic. Fighting monsters, saving a ruined village, even finding your egg. Like a story, the kind where the hero just has to do his best, be honorable and good, and he wins. We'd all win."

"Then take a bow and watch the curtain fall?" Cerisse asked. He nodded, and she laughed. The sound was so unexpected that it brought a flush of blood to Jace's cheeks.

"Don't laugh at me!" he shouted, more angrily than he'd meant.

Cerisse fell silent. She shook her head, the auburn braid waggling behind her back. "Jace, I'm not laughing at you. I'm trying to explain." She sighed, letting go of his hand to tug at her braid in irritation.

"Life isn't a performance," Belen said. "You don't get to try again if you drop a ball you're juggling, or if you forget a line or a step in the dance. You just have to keep going, even if someone gets hurt. You have to do the right thing because you can't be certain what the outcome will be, so you have to at least be certain that you can look back on your own actions and know you didn't give in to evil."

Jace looked down at his mud-covered boots, remembering the feeling of flight between Belen's giant silver wings. Had it been so different from falling? When he knew the ground was rushing up to meet him, with no way to save himself, wasn't that flight too? Do what's right, Belen said. No matter what the cost or whether you'll win or lose.

Otherwise, how could he live with himself? "You're right, Belen," he said quietly.

"Psst, Jace," Cerisse volunteered, a mischievous glint in her eye. "You can win, if you know how."

Both Belen and Jace stared at her. "Uh . . . how?" Jace asked. He wasn't entirely sure he wanted to know the answer.

"You can win," she repeated, "if you don't care what the prize will be. You can't say, 'If I get such a thing, or if I see that, then I win.' And you certainly can't say, 'If I make so-and-so love me, I win.' " Her smile faded. "That's not winning, that's asking life to bribe you." Her eyes glanced from Jace to Belen and back again. "If what you want doesn't happen, that has to be fine too. No matter who gets hurt or what you have to do, if you know you've done the right thing—even if what you want doesn't happen—then you win. That's the only way to live."

"Is that right, Cerisse?" Belen asked, a strangeness in her voice.

Cerisse shrugged off the question. "Chin up, Jace. Listen to me. What we're going to do is climb up those bars, go out onto the roof, and find Ebano. Then we'll all talk to Mysos, and the wizard will have to listen to us. He'll have to let Belen stay."

"I thought you just said you couldn't decide what the prize will be." Jace tried to smile.

"I haven't," she answered with a wink. "I've set our strategy. It's not the same thing. After all we've been through and sacrificed, Mysos will have no other choice.

He's a white-robed wizard, after all, and they're supposed to be good, kind people. If we trust that Belen's a good person because she's a silver dragon, then the same thing holds true for white-robed wizards, right?" She and Jace shared a smile.

Belen climbed back over to the bars and began to scale them, leaving faint red marks where her hands gripped the broken wooden boards. Jace stood beneath her, helping to balance the dancer's light steps until she could pull herself out onto the roof. With a smile, she reached back and gripped Cerisse's hand, helping the half-elf through with a tug. The girls paused on the roof while Jace jumped up to grab the wooden planking, exchanging quiet words. He jerked himself up as he would on the high wire, climbing with his the sheer strength of his arms. "Little help here?" he gasped, flopping chest first on the roof and kicking his legs weakly. The two girls turned quickly and reached for him. Cerisse laughed nervously and they pulled him all the way up.

It was nice to be out in the open again, breathing clean air that didn't stink of hay and animals. Jace took a deep breath, letting his body grow accustomed to the feeling of sun on his skin. A sound reached him, tickling his ears until he turned to look off the edge of the wagon roof and follow it. "Hey," he said. "What are all those people yelling about?"

"Oh my gosh, Jace." Cerisse grabbed his arm, pointing. "There's a fight over in the clearing behind the big top. Someone's hurt!" Her face paled, and she jerked her arm back to cover her mouth. "That body on the ground . . . at the White Robe's feet. That looks like . . . Ebano."

CHAPTER THIRTEEN

They pushed through the small crowd around the clearing, careful to hide themselves among the circus performers who were whispering and muttering. In the center of the clearing, the ground was cracked and blackened, stained with poisonous acid and broken open by magical force. Mysos, the White Robe, stood over the fallen mesmerist, his hands clenched in angry fists. "In Paladine's name!" he roared. "What is going on? Who is this man? Why did he attack me?"

Worver pushed through the bystanders, shooing them away with sweeping gestures. "Stand back, good people. I'm sure there's been some sort of misunderstanding." He shoved aside Bobbo and one of the other clowns to come to a clucking halt beside the White Robe of Palanthas. "That's Ebano! He's our master mesmerist—a hypnotist beyond compare."

Jace could see Worver twisting his mustache around

one finger while his strange monkey jumped from shoulder to shoulder. "Attacked you, you say?"

Ebano lay face down, spread out on the ground between them. His dark robes were scorched by the acid. The air had the pungent stench of singed fabric and burned flesh. Jace wanted to get a better look at Ebano's wounds, but there was no way to find out if the mesmerist was still alive without risking Worver seeing them among the crowd. They'd have to wait and see.

"He came to my wagon, wouldn't stop pounding on it, and when I answered, he used magic on me. Illegal magic, I'd imagine." Mysos scowled. "He's certainly never been to any Tower of High Sorcery that I've ever known."

"Well, that is something! Used real magic, hmm? I'd never have believed it. I thought his whole hocus-pocus thing was just sleight of hand." Worver's pet, Tsusu, leaped down to the ground and started poking at Ebano, leaning in close to see if the dark-skinned mesmerist was still breathing. The scaly little monkey jerked back and started chittering. "Still breathing?" Worver asked his pet. "I see."

Cerisse gripped Jace's arm. "Ebano's alive!"

Jace hushed her quietly, shooting her a smile.

"Perhaps he was under some sort of spell when he attacked you." Worver smoothed his mustache.

"A spell?" Mysos barked. "Are there more illegal wizards among your performers?"

"What? No!" Waving his hands in distress, Worver protested, "That's not what I meant! I meant, you see . . . that perhaps one of the mesmerist's spells backfired. He might have been cruelly manipulated by his own magical mental control, some dark hypnotism. Or perhaps one of his recent subjects took the joke poorly, you see, and came back to cause him trouble. It wasn't any of us! Yes, I'm sure that's what happened. Poor Ebano. How tragic."

"Wasn't this one of the men who went with the dragon?" Mysos's sharp eyes took in everything, flicking from the dancing monkey to Worver's uncomfortable shifting. "How is it that he has returned and she has not?"

Stumped, Worver glanced back and forth among the performers, trying to look anywhere but at Mysos's face. "Well, ah, perhaps he was sent ahead . . . to tell us how they're doing?"

"We have to get Ebano out of there," Jace whispered to Cerisse. "If you cause a distraction, he'll have to notice. Maybe open the horses' pen so he has to stop them from getting out? That might give me a chance to grab Ebano, get him out of here, and tend to his wounds. It's not a very good plan, but I don't have any other ideas."

"Do you think binding his wounds will help?" Belen asked softly.

"Maybe. I can't tell how bad he's hurt." Jace cursed under his breath, glad that they had stopped by the big top to pick up their things. The short sword at his belt felt very reassuring right now. "Do we have another option?"

"If you want a distraction," Cerisse brightened, "I can do that."

"All right." He shared a smile with Cerisse. Impulsively, she reached out and grabbed his hand, squeezing it gently. It made him feel better, being close to her, like he wasn't so alone in all this trouble. He wrapped his fingers around Cerisse's for a moment. "While you get the horses, Belen and I will . . . wait, hang on. Where's Belen?" Panicked, he dropped Cerisse's hand and lunged upward, looking around at the crowd in horrified realization.

Belen had moved away from them to the center of the crowd. Before he could yell out her name or get her attention, Belen stepped into the clearing. She faced Worver and Mysos with almost regal calm. "I have returned," she said simply. All eyes locked on her. Jace could see the open confusion of the clowns, Mysos's relieved half smile, and Worver's grin of hysteria.

"This man is a companion of mine." She gestured to Ebano. "Can his wounds be healed?"

Worver strode to Belen's side and took her elbow, pulling her close. "Belen, my dear! There you are! It's so good to see that you're all right!" From where he stood, Jace could see that Worver's grip was far too tight for comfort. To answer the lady's question, Mysos took a moment to kneel next to Ebano and inspect the fallen man's burned robes and pained skin. While he was looking at Ebano, Worver was trying to drag Belen away. When the ringmaster spoke, his voice was low and quiet so Mysos wouldn't hear him. "I assume our little friends are roaming about?"

"No," Belen said clearly. "They're dead."

"What is she doing?" Cerisse gasped, holding tightly to Jace's arm.

"She's protecting us. If Worver thinks we're alive, he'll have to keep trying to kill us. Now get down, he'll see us." Jace grabbed Cerisse's shoulder and pushed her back, ducking quickly behind a pile of feed bags.

Worver tugged on Belen again, trying to maneuver her toward his red wagon. Unwilling to be moved even an inch, Belen jerked her arm out of the ringmaster's grip and glared at him.Worver started to speak, but Belen cut him off, demanding, "Can you heal Ebano, Worver?"

"What?" Worver blinked. "I don't know what you mean, my dear—"

She cut him off again, her eyes flashing. "You healed

Hautos when he was hurt by the werewolves. You healed Francis the Firebreather. Others. Can you heal Ebano?"

"Minor incidents! Petty injuries!" Worver said loudly, waving his hand in dismissal. He pitched his voice low again and hissed, "I don't see any reason to help Ebano since he has attacked our guest." Worver's eyebrows flew up and down like butterflies. "I would be better served if I let him die, poor fellow. Unless, of course, you'd be willing to make it worth my while?" His eyes flicked over the crowd and his voice dropped so low that Jace could barely make it out. "I'd so much rather have you part of the circus *willingly*, dear girl, but I'll take the best I can get."

Belen bit her lip, looking down at Ebano. Mysos was shaking his head somberly as he looked at the dark-skinned mesmerist's wounds. Ebano's body lay broken and crumpled on the sandy ground. Jace knew immediately what Belen was thinking. She wouldn't give her word unless she meant it.

"I'll do it." Belen's voice was heavy, weighed down by defeat.

Worver relaxed visibly and broke into a smile. "There, there, my dear Belen. A tragedy, I know, but I shall make every endeavor to see that you are well cared for. But you've gotten out of all that trouble, and you're here! Wonderful.

I see that the experience has educated you. Very good, my dear. Then there's nothing else between us. Now, tell me, do you promise not to make trouble? To let bygones be bygones?" The ringmaster's tone sharpened slightly.

"I will—if you heal Ebano."

"A trade, my dear? Very well. If I heal Ebano of these wounds, you will stay. You'll sign the legal contracts with the White Robe that will make me officially your caretaker? You won't cause trouble?" No one else seemed to be paying much attention to the ringmaster. Their attention was focused on Mysos and the fallen Ebano.

Belen faced Worver squarely. "You have an agreement, you beast. Now make good on your part of the deal."

Worver smiled and stepped away. "Mysos, is he alive?"

The White Robe looked deeply concerned. "Yes. I'm no healer, but these wounds are significant. I don't know if he will recover, and if he does, I'm afraid he will be crippled by the injuries." Mysos's hand lingered on Ebano's unmoving shoulder. "I am sorry, my friend, for whatever insult I did you that brought you to this end."

Worver bowed, fluffing out his short cloak and doffing his top hat. "This is a circus, my lord Mysos. You'd be amazed at the recovery time of even the most serious wounds. Our healers are well trained to deal with injury garnered while performing our amazing feats." The ring-master spun on his heel, never letting go of Belen's elbow. "Hautos, my horned companion! Come here and gather this poor fellow. The rest of you, go back to your duties—the crowd hasn't left the big top, and we've little time to spare gawking about. Go on now, go on."

The minotaur stepped out from the crowd. He flexed his tremendous muscles and made soft gruff sounds in response to the ringmaster's commands. When he walked past Mysos, the wizard stiffened. "You're quite sure every-thing will be fine?" asked the White Robe.

"Yes, yes, trust me on that." Worver tried to take Mysos's arm as he'd taken Belen's, but the White Robe pulled away and brushed off his sleeve where the ringmaster had touched it. "Now, then, why don't you and I and the lady Belen step into my wagon? I'm sure you must be very interested in her trip."

"Yes, I am. And I have those contracts you'd mentioned, the magical ones that will enforce our agree-ment. Assuming the lady is agreed, that is, and that she has no further information that will change the situation." He looked at Belen sternly.

"No, none," she answered, her silver hair flowing over her shoulders as she walked toward the wagon. "I went to Angvale, but there was no one there. I . . . I did attack the village. I deserve to be punished, and I surrender myself to it without argument."

Mysos looked impressed, even if his brows were still knitted. He nodded once for emphasis, and then turned toward the wagon.

"Fine, just fine, that's settled, then." Worver tossed a look back over his shoulder. Hautos was hefting Ebano, pitching him face first over his bull-sized shoulder with a snort. Worver smiled sweetly. "Hautos, you know what to do?" He stepped aside, hand on the minotaur's shoulder, and gave him some whispered directions. The smooth smile never left the ringmaster's face.

The minotaur snorted deprecatingly, little shots of steam whistling past the big brass ring in his nose. He carried Ebano off, glowering at anyone brave enough to take even a single step to follow. Worver led Belen and Mysos into his wagon as the crowd slowly began to disperse, uneasy whispers floating among the performers.

"Oh, Jace." Cerisse wiped at her face with a sleeve, leaving a dirty smudge along her cheekbone. "We can't let her sign those papers! If she does, that horrible Worver will have won, and Belen will literally be his slave. She'll belong to the circus like some sort of property!"

"Yeah, and who says that he'll only use her for the circus? With a dragon on his side, Worver could do a lot worse—and use the circus to cover up all the things he does. This is awful."

"Can't we go in there and stop it?"

"No. Not until Ebano's all right." Jace sighed. "Belen knows that this is the only chance Ebano has to be healed. We've got to follow Hautos, help Ebano, and then come back and save her."

"Then we'd better do it fast. Belen will keep her word. She's too good a person to break it, even if Worver's a stinking cheat." Cerisse bit her lip. "So what do we do?"

Gloomy and angry, Jace thumbed over his shoulder. "We follow Hautos. If he can't heal Ebano, then the whole thing's off and I'm going to go right into that wagon and tell Mysos everything—no matter what happens to me."

"Jace!" Cerisse's faded smile regained a bit of its certainty. "You'd do that? But it's dangerous—Worver wouldn't think twice about killing you. He didn't hesitate to throw us in that cage."

"I don't care." Jace's stomach sank a bit. Cerisse was right. Despite the fact that he'd been brave—they'd all been brave!—against the werewolves, the chimera, and a hundred little dangers along the way, this was different. Heroes didn't get blackmailed.

"You must really care about Belen." The little dirt smudge on Cerisse's cheek had grown larger, a brush of damp brown dust against her lightly tanned skin. "I think it's great that she has a friend like you, Jace, who would go through so much to help her out. No matter what, you're there for her. You always have been."

"You did the same thing." He tried to keep the minotaur in sight, waiting until the beast was several steps away before he started moving. "You went with us to protect her and help her out. That's what good friends do."

"I wasn't—" Cerisse stopped and shook her head. "What I'm trying to say is that I hope . . . well, I hope that everything works out for both of you, Jace."

"It will, I promise. No matter what Worver tries, we'll find a way to stop him. Look! Hautos ducked behind the sharpshooter game." Jace pointed. "We'd better hurry."

Cerisse looked away. "Yeah, we'd better catch up before he has a chance to do anything despicable. I don't trust that minotaur." Jace nodded, and they trotted quickly after the strongman. Hautos was easy to track—he didn't bother to skulk, and he was far too big to hide behind anything smaller than an elephant or a fully loaded wagon. He walked through the circus, away from the big top, toward the wagons that usually held the stores and extra tent canvases. "Where is he going?"

Jace squinted. "Not toward any of the herbalists, that's for sure. Duck!" They jumped behind one of the many-spoked wheels of a large wagon. The minotaur swung his heavy head back and forth, looking around for witnesses. He shuffled Ebano over his shoulder, evoking a soft groan from the wounded man, and then strode directly toward a small, shabby-looking wagon off to the side. While they watched, Hautos reached for a big brass key at his belt and unlocked a heavy wooden door at the rear of the wagon. After opening it, he tossed Ebano inside with a callousness that made Jace wince. After another scathing look around the wagon, the minotaur climbed inside. "Jace, look! The wagon didn't move when he climbed inside."

"So?"

Cerisse rolled her eyes. "You may be a tightrope walker, but I guess you don't know anything about balancing. If something as big and heavy as a minotaur climbs on one end of a tightrope, the whole thing slopes toward it, right?"

He blinked, startled. "You're right! But it didn't! So there must be something equally heavy in the wagon that kept it level despite Hautos's weight—like a big, solid rock."

They crept up on the wagon, slipping closer as Hautos slammed the heavy door. "Look!" Jace whispered.

Ropes slid up from the ground, weaving tightly against the door. A small series of stones rolled forward too, piling themselves against the steps hanging from the back of the wagon. If they stepped on the stair, a stone would fall with a tinkling sound and warn Hautos. "What's happening?" Jace asked.

"It's the circus helpers, the ones who fill the chalk bins and tidy up the ropes. They're helping him!"

"Circus helpers? I thought that was just some sort of magic."

"Did you ever notice how the circus doesn't pay anyone to help out, but all the grunt work gets done anyway? Most people just ignore it or assume it's some minor prestidigitation by one of the workers, but I never did. I call them the 'circus helpers.' I saw one once, and it looked like a little white sparrow. Sort of small, winged. When it saw me looking, it vanished."

"You know, you're right. I didn't really think about it at the time. I just assumed they'd always been here." Jace froze, grabbing her hand. "How many years ago did you start noticing them, Cerisse?"

"Oh, about five." She rolled her eyes, making the connection. "You're right. It was just about the time Belen came. Right after Angvale was attacked."

"He's the one who lied to Belen and stole the village stone." It all made sense. Jace ground his teeth in anger. First the werewolves, now Belen, and now the stone. Worver was far more evil than Jace had given him credit for being. "I think we can get close enough to the side of this wagon to peek inside. Maybe we can see what Hautos is doing in there."

Jace moved quietly, slipping across the dusty clearing between wagons until he reached the heavy one with the minotaur inside. Cerisse followed him, keeping an eye out for anyone else who might catch them in the act. They crept to the side of the wagon and pulled themselves up to the windowsill to catch a glimpse inside through the open shutters.

There was Hautos, kneeling over Ebano, whom he had placed on a blanket on the floor. The minotaur was removing a corner of a thick gray blanket from a tall lump wrapped in protective ropes. The blanket fell away slowly, revealing white stone beneath. Jace could see that the surface was covered in delicate tracery carved into the stone by a master hand. There were etchings of vines, flowers, and birds on the stone that looked so real Jace thought they might flap their wings and fly away when the minotaur got too close. A soft, faint glow emanated from the rock, luminous like night blossoms in the moonlight. The minotaur snorted and lifted Ebano's arm to check his pulse. Dropping the limp arm, the minotaur started digging through Ebano's pockets and found a small amount of money in a leather bag.

"I thought minotaurs were supposed to be honorable," Cerisse snarked.

"Sssh," Jace hissed. If Hautos heard them . . . but no, the minotaur was far too interested in the bag of money he'd taken from the hypnotist's sleeve. Apparently satisfied, the minotaur grabbed Ebano's hand again and pressed it to the stone. A soft brightness washed out from the stone, covering Ebano like a blanket. Hautos stepped away quickly and watched, his big dark eyes absorbing the radiance.

"What's happening?"

"Look at his back!" Jace shushed her. "His wounds are healing!"

Indeed, the scorched and blackened flesh along Ebano's back was turning pink again, the charred velvet of his robes fluttering away from lacerations caused by acid all along his spine. Where the sickening ivory of bone had shown through, muscle and sinew were knitting together again. And his breathing, once labored and faint, deepened with a shuddering rush. Although his clothes were still ragged and ruined, the hypnotist's body was recovering at an astounding rate. The stone was healing him, feeding the flame of his life and slowly encouraging it to flare up again.

In the phosphorescent light of the stone's radiance, Jace began to make out other figures, small and delicate, clustered around Ebano. Barely taller than Jace's forearm, they were tugging at Ebano's robes, pulling the edges away from the wounds. One carried silken thread and lanced the lacerations, stitching the skin together as one might sew up a blanket. Where the thread settled against the mesmerist's skin, it sank in and vanished, leaving perfect, unmarred flesh in its wake.

"What are those?" This time, it was Jace's turn to risk the whisper. Cerisse gave a mystified shrug, staring in awe. There were several of the little creatures fluttering about the stone now, one carrying a thimbleful of water to the fallen man's lips, another delicately scraping away dead flesh on the worst of the burns to reveal fresh, newly grown skin beneath. Jace and Cerisse gaped.

"Those are the circus helpers! Spirits of the stone! The fairies are doing all the work around here. Ooh, that steams me!" Cerisse lowered herself, unable to watch any more. "My mother told me stories of the fairies that lived in the woods when she was a child. Worver, you filthy, stinking, horrible man! You've enslaved them the same way you're going to enslave Belen!"

Jace dropped down beside her, crouching behind the wagon's wheel. "Poor things. They probably serve whoever has control of the stone. They don't have a choice," Jace guessed. He rubbed his chin. "That's why the circus makes so much money. He doesn't pay laborers, and nobody can see the fairies unless they're near the stone, so nobody complains. I bet that's why he stole Chislev's stone in the first place."

There was a soft moan from within the wagon. Jace snuck back up, peering over the windowsill again to see the mesmerist lifting his head from the floor with a bemused expression. Grunting, Hautos reached for a rope coiled nearby and drew it out, wrapping it around Ebano's body with ruthless efficiency. Too weak and confused to do more than protest in his odd foreign language, Ebano was quickly tied down. Hautos pulled a long knife from his belt and held it near the mesmerist's eye. "You healed so we can show dragon lady. You try to get away, I kill you. You make too much noise, I kill you. Pretty much, you do anything at all, I kill you. You do nothing. Soon Worver will tell me, and I kill you anyway. Just a matter of time, you stupid no-language finger waggler. Understand?" Whether Ebano understood or not, the threat of the knife passing back and forth a few inches from his nose seemed to have gotten the minotaur's point across.

"Why, that rotten minotaur! Do you think he'll really hurt Ebano?" Cerisse reached for one of the three darts she had salvaged from the fight with the arcox and started to head for the door of the wagon. Jace grabbed her shoulder, shoving her back against the wagon.

"Stop! We can't beat Hautos. He can lift an elephant over his head!"

"Yeah, but he's about as smart as a board." Cerisse pushed back, making Jace step away. "They're going to kill Ebano anyway, and if we can help him get free, he can use magic on the minotaur. We just have to distract Hautos long enough to untie Ebano and make sure he's all right."

Fair point. As annoying as Cerisse was sometimes, she could always be counted on to find a way out of a bad situation. "All right. I'll get Hautos's attention and make him chase me. You slip into the wagon and untie Ebano. Ready?"

Cerisse had no time to argue because the wagon door was opening. Jace winked at her and lunged out into the clearing to face the minotaur as the heavy strongman was stepping outside. "You know, Hautos, I always knew you were stupid. I just didn't know how stupid. Do you really do everything Worver tells you? I swear, if I didn't know better, I'd think you really were one of the circus oxen. Do you pull wagons too?"

The minotaur's nostrils flared, his head surging up to stare Jace in the eye. Jace doubted anyone had ever spoken to the hugely muscular, tremendously strong Hautos this way before. Hautos charged down the stairs toward him with an ear-splitting bellow.

Jace fled, feet pounding the earth with all of his might. His advantage was his speed—the minotaur was notoriously slow, and his hooves didn't have the traction of Jace's boots. The boy put on a burst of speed, hoping to get a wide berth between himself and Hautos's fists. The minotaur was in full chase, barely able to make words as he raged behind Jace. Jace ducked around wagons, dived over booths, and dodged behind the guess-your-weight machine, Hautos only steps behind. He heard shrieks from performers jumping out of the way and nearly ran over some of the halfling cannoneers. "Move! Move! Move!" he shouted at them as he leaped over their heads. They shouted angrily after him, but their cries were cut short from being bowled over and nearly skewered on Hautos's horns.

Jace's breath was coming in short, gasping puffs. His thighs hurt from trying to stay ahead of the minotaur, and he had already circled the lion cages twice in the hopes of losing him, but Hautos wasn't about to be shaken from his prey. Jace tried to lose him among the flapping laundry of the horseback riders, but Hautos tore down the fluttering cloaks and left them in piles on the ground. Gathering his strength, Jace dodged in and out among the firebreathers, yelping as he moved too close to their practice and singed off the top of his hair. Again, Hautos wasn't deterred, charging through the braziers of hot coals with no thought at all to his own well-being.

Hautos might be stupid, Jace thought, but he sure was stubborn.

There! Up ahead! I might be able to lose him behind that red wagon.

Then Jace realized that red wagon was *the* red wagon—the one he'd run from in the first place. Ebano and Cerisse were climbing down the stairs, completely unaware that Jace was running toward them, trailing a horned sledgehammer of wrath. Jace had only enough breath to shout their names, hoping they could duck aside before Hautos saw them.

Too late.

If Jace thought the minotaur was angered at being called stupid, it was nothing to how he reacted when he saw Ebano escaping. Hautos's eyes reddened, his jaw clenched, and Jace thought he actually saw steam coming out of the strongman's nostrils.

"Ebano says he has no spells!" Cerisse shouted in terror. "We've got nothing!"

Well, it was a good try. Jace threw himself past the wagon opening, desperate to find anything that would pull the minotaur's attention from the others. Hautos had changed directions, piling on speed as he charged the wagon door. "Cerisse! Get out of his way!"

She clambered up the stairs, scrabbling out of the minotaur's path. Ebano moved with her, but never took his eyes off the charging minotaur.

Cerisse started throwing things—laundry, juggling pins, wagon equipment—anything she could reach inside the wagon. Hautos ignored her and kept after Jace, bawling from the depths of his belly. Fingers brushing Jace's tunic, the minotaur hurled himself full speed up the steps of the red wagon. Jace spun and drew his sword from his belt, ready to let the minotaur pound him to a pulp in order to save his friends.

Hautos practically flew up the three steps to the wagon's door, stepped through the doorway, and ran face first into a thick iron skillet. The minotaur staggered, knees quaking. He took a half step backward, missed the stair, and fell. He landed flat on his back, a little poof of dust swirling around him. His eyes crossed and his tongue lolled from his mouth.

The velvet-robed mesmerist stepped out onto the stair, crossing the frying pan over his chest as if it were a sacred weapon. He gave Jace a very stern stare. "Surprise," he intoned somberly, "is best magic."

CHAPTER FOURTEEN

"C an you hear me?" Jace whispered into the wagon's darkness. Cerisse had pulled the window nearly shut so that none of the passing circus performers would overhear them. Hautos was tied up and left on a cot they'd uncovered amid the random storage items that took up most of the wagon.

While she and Ebano had been triple and quadruple knotting those ropes, Jace had taken the time to untie the stone, removing all of the covers that had hidden it and revealing the glistening white surface. It was covered with small carvings, so lifelike that Jace thought the wings on one of the birds might beat at any moment. The craftsmanship was beautiful, beyond anything he'd ever seen. "Can you hear me?" he asked again.

There was a soft stirring in the air, and the stone began to softly glow. It was faint, like the twinkling of a single candle spread out along the length of the marble. The stone itself was large, almost as tall as Jace, and as thick as the length from Jace's wrist to his elbow. Jace's hand lingered over a carving of a small fox inquisitively slinking through twined underbrush. The fur was detailed, each tuft painstakingly worked into the stone. The fox crept down a forest road near a village symbolized by thatched roofs peeking through the trees. "Angvale," Jace said, remembering the ruined town.

A weight landed on his shoulder, something light and gentle.

"Home." The voice was thready and soft. A sigh tinkled like tiny silvery bells.

Jace tried not to jump at the sound of it. He turned his head slowly to look at the little being crouching on his shoulder. It was small, hardly as long as his forearm if it stood up straight. Gossamer wings flickered and trailed behind it like silk in the wind, and its face was beautiful, if filled with a keen sadness.

"Jace," Cerisse muttered, "stand very still. You have a fairy on you."

"I know." He smiled. "What do I do?"

Cerisse rubbed her temples, squeezing her eyes shut. "Mom told me that you should feed fairies to show them you're friendly. So . . . give it something to eat?"

"Food. Right." Jace stared at her. On his shoulder, the

fairy shifted and moaned softly. A faint shimmery dust trickled down from its glistening wings. Jace dropped his voice to a whisper. "What does it eat?"

"I'm trying to remember." Cerisse looked from Jace to Ebano, but for once, the usually placid mesmerist seemed as baffled as they. "Milk or honey?" she guessed. "Sweets?"

"I have some crackers left from breakfast. Maybe it'd like them." Slowly, Jace pulled a cracker out of his belt pouch and held it up to the fairy. "Hey," Jace said in as soothing a tone as he could muster. "Want a cracker?"

The fairy looked at it skeptically, wings fluttering with more little tinkling sounds. Jace held it between forefinger and thumb and pushed it closer to the little fairy balanced on his shoulder. Jace held his breath.

The tiny creature sniffed, peered, scrabbled forward, and finally reached out delicately and took it. "Thank you." Its silvery voice was a bit stilted from underuse, but something in the incredibly polite tone reminded Jace of Belen.

"You're very welcome," Jace stammered.

Only after the pleasantries were done did the fairy eat—and it ate ravenously, stuffing its face with grunts and eager smacks as cracker crumbs dusted Jace's tunic. A shiver ran through it and it gazed at Jace with tremendous gratitude, brushing a wingtip against his cheek.

Two more appeared in the air over the stone and a

third fluttered to a perch atop Cerisse's auburn hair. They made soft noises and gestured toward Jace's belt pouch with grasping little hands. "Are they all hungry?" Jace scrambled to pull out a few more crackers, offering one to each of the little creatures. "I only have a few crackers left. I hope it's enough. These fairies act like they're starving."

"Pukah," the one on Jace's shoulder trilled. "We are pukah. Chislev's friends. Servants of the stone." It sounded intelligent, and even better, friendly.

"How many of you are there?"

"Six."

Six little pukah? To do the chores and grunt work for an entire circus? "My name is Jace. These are my friends, Cerisse and Ebano. Oh . . . you've probably seen us before, since you work for Worver."

At the sound of the ringmaster's name, the fairies hissed and snarled, their wings buzzing like angry bees. Jace backpedaled. "We aren't here for Worver. We're here because we're trying to help Belen. We went to the village of Angvale."

Hearing the town's name, the pukah calmed down, and the one on Jace's shoulder sat back with a sigh.

"Home. We miss it. Please . . . can you take us home?"

Jace smiled. "We'd love to if we can. But first we

need to know more about the stone. Can you move it? Does Worver have a way to control it, or does he have power over it just because he 'owns' it?" He struggled to think of questions that had come so easily when he was thinking this plan up.

The pukah settled down all around the wagon, on windowsills, shoulders and other perches. The one on Cerisse's shoulder was slowly unweaving her braid, letting the hair slide through her lithe fingers. The little fellow sitting on Jace's shoulder appeared to be the leader, or at least, the most talkative, and it was the one to answer. "Where stone goes, we go. Who owns stone, owns us. So Chislev bound us, so we serve."

"Owns it? So, if I pick it up and take it—"

The fey creature shook its head. "No. *Owns* it." The pukah gestured toward its neck, scratching lightly at the luminescent skin. "Makes us come. Makes us do."

"He's got some sort of necklace? Something that ties him to the stone and makes him the one who can command you? All right, we can handle that. So all we've got to do is get that necklace and then take it and the stone back to Angvale. Simple." Jace beamed, pleased with his logic.

Cerisse shook her head. "Plus, rescue Belen from Worver's blackmail, free the pukah, and explain everything to the White Robe. Not so simple."

She was right. Worver had Belen and whatever necklace controlled the pukah, and he was currently spinning Mysos whatever tale would get him the most benefit. As much as Jace wanted to take the stone and run, it wouldn't do them any good. A hero would go and face Worver directly, fight him one on one, and then sweep Belen up and tell her that everything would be all right, everything would be wonderful. She'd be so happy, so excited that she might just—

Cerisse jabbed Jace in the side with her elbow, triggering a sharp surge of pain. Jace choked, coughing and clutching his injured ribcage. "Hey!" he yelped. The pukah leaped off Jace's shoulder with a squeal. "That hurt!"

"Oh! You are hurt?" The pukah cocked its head, hovering up and down above Jace's shoulder. "I fix." It swooped down over the stone, landing on the rugged top with a gentle graze. It stood awkwardly atop the rough stone, reaching out for Jace's hand with both of its small, delicate ones. Atop Cerisse's head, the one that had been playing with her braid began squawking and tugging on her hair, gesturing for her to do the same. "Come here, I will fix all."

Remembering how Ebano's terrible wound had been restored, Jace lifted his hand and reached out three fingers to the pukah. Cerisse did the same, following his lead. Ebano smiled. The pukah grabbed Jace's fingers in one hand, and Cerisse's in the other, and closed its eyes. With a swoosh, everything turned as white as snow. Brilliant, flaming light blinded Jace, turning the world pale and glittery. He didn't remember Ebano's healing causing this much glare, but then again, perhaps this was how healing looked from the inside. He heard Cerisse gasp as warmth flooded over them, wrapping them in comfort and joy. The stone radiated life and love as much as a mother's hug or his father's smile. Jace laughed out loud, feeling it deep in his bones, and somehow he knew that everything was going to be all right.

When the light faded, the chief of the pukah was on his shoulder, smiling blissfully at him. Jace's ribs didn't hurt anymore, and he didn't even feel hungry. Jace grinned and then realized his hand was still outstretched—and his fingers were entwined with Cerisse's over the stone. Her hand was warm and sturdy, calloused from juggling but still soft to the touch. It felt . . . nice.

Jace jerked his hand away and blushed. Cerisse flexed her fingers, untying the bandage that bound her forearm. The wound where the chimera had hurt her was nothing more than a thin red line tracing the contour of her bone. Her fingers moved freely without any sign of poison or stiffness. "Amazing."

"Hang on!" Startled, Jace waved his hand at the little creature, causing it to do loops in the air around his fingers. "You healed us!"

The pukah stared at him as if Jace had suddenly turned into cheese. It avoided Jace's swoops with a cheerful trill, flipping between his palms and doing backflips in the air. Jace felt a weight lift off his conscience. "Now we have to stop Worver from enslaving Belen the same way he's enslaved the pukah," he said.

Cerisse frowned. "We've got to stop her from signing that document."

"That won't be easy," Jace mused. "Belen promised to sign the contract. She going to go through with her promise because she gave her word. We have to stop *Mysos* from signing it!"

The juggler's eyes widened. "You're right. Either way, though, we've got to get there fast and . . . and . . . uh... fix the . . . uh, fight the . . . uh . . . help me out here."

"Do something." Jace finished her sentence. "Yeah, that's the hard part. Still, we may be working without a net again, but this time I'm not afraid." He grinned at her. "I'm also not alone."

"I'm not afraid either, Jace." She beamed. "Let's go."

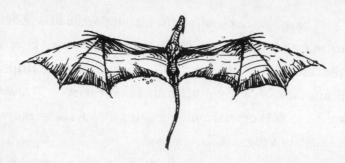

Chapter Fifteen

Jace and Cerisse crept up to the ringmaster's red wagon with Ebano in tow, darting from hiding spot to hiding spot along the way. When they got there, they hid beneath the window as they'd done before, listening carefully and peering in to watch those inside. Jace hushed Cerisse again, wishing that she could just calm down for once in her life, and kept an eye on the proceedings. In order for their plan to work, they had to wait until Belen had fulfilled her word—or else she'd work against them out of honor.

"Ebano needs a moment to rest," Cerisse told him. "His wounds and that fight against Mysos took a lot out of him."

"All right. He can sit here behind these barrels. I'll keep an eye on what's going on inside, and we'll go in as soon as he's ready."

Ebano nodded and tried to catch his breath. The mystic's dark skin was sallow, his steps weary. If this turned into a fight—and knowing Worver it would—Jace would need Ebano to be as rested as possible. Cerisse had picked up a few throwing darts along the way, and now tested their tips with a steady smile.

"Don't take too long," Jace told them. "We have to get Belen out of there before the contract is fully signed."

Ebano sat back, crossing his arms and legs. Within a moment, his eyes were closed, his lips moving in breathless prayer. Whatever he was doing, his color was improving, and the shaking in his hands was beginning to ease. Jace risked another peep into Worver's wagon, trying to gauge how long they had before it was too late.

"Now, Master Mysos, if you will simply sign this official contract certifying that I am Belen's guardian and completely in charge of her rehabilitation, we can consider the matter resolved." Worver took the quill from Belen's hand and blew on her signature, scattering a bit of sand over the paper to dry the ink. The mage was tapping his fingers on the table top, staring at Belen intently and ignoring Worver's fumbling hands. The ringmaster placed the contract, ink, and quill directly in front of the mage.

Belen sat quietly, hands folded in her lap, head bowed. She hadn't argued even once during the entire procedure, from Worver's wheedling to Mysos's stoic recitation of her crimes against the village of Angvale. When Worver announced the deal he had been hoping for, Mysos had expected to hear her either approve or disapprove—but she'd sat there in silence. "When I sign this," Mysos informed her once more, "you will be magically bound. You will be tied to its terms. You will remain here among the circus folk, and you will work off your debt to society as we see fit, through giving away your salary, assisting Worver with his charity performances, and the like. Beyond that, you will have no freedoms. You will have no independence. Should you leave the circus or fail to provide payment for your crimes, you will be hunted down and destroyed by all of the White Robes of Palanthas."

"Exactly how long did you say this contract would be good, master mage?" Worver sidled up to him with the pen and ink.

"One year for every resident of that tragic, lost village."

"And, er, how long is that, if you don't mind?"

"There were seventy-three residents lost when the village of Angvale was attacked." Mysos asserted.

"Seventy-three years, you say!" Worver pressed the quill into Mysos's hand and then sat forward in his leather-covered traveling chair. "Plenty of time, plenty of time. The circus will be rich!" Worver was practically glowing. "I mean, rich at heart!" he amended quickly under Mysos's glare. "With a great deal of money given to the poor and homeless in Palanthas, of course."

"Hmph. Of course." Mysos tapped the quill against the parchment, scraping the surface slightly. "Belen, you are agreed?"

She nodded.

Mysos hesitated, and Worver wheedled, "Is something wrong, my dear wizard?"

The pen wavered above the paper. "It seems something of a waste to leave a dragon to dance for pennies, but the judgment is fair, and the contract is legal according to the law in Palanthas. If this is the punishment that Belen wants, then I am willing to be reasonable, as she did turn herself in for the crimes. The best punishment must be one that serves the community and betters the lives of others."

"Yes, yes, that's exactly right!" Worver crowed, pushing subtly against Mysos's wrist. The mage glared at him and jerked away, making the ringmaster shrink back. "Let me get you a glass of water, sir. That'll quench your thirst. Justice—it's a thirsty business!"

Jace grimaced. Thirstiness wasn't the reason Mysos was hesitating, if Jace was any judge of the mage's character. What made him pause was the greedy leer in the ringmaster's smile. The White Robe was trying to think of other options. Mysos couldn't afford to stay here and watch over Belen, and despite his bluff, if the dragon refused to come to Palanthas, it would take more than just one wizard to force her. This deal, distasteful as it was, fulfilled all the requirements of law, and Mysos knew it.

Jace hoped that the wizard would be equally happy to be offered another way out of the deal. "That's it, that's all the time we have. We've got to go now." He shook Ebano's shoulder. "He's about to sign!"

"Very well, then." Mysos began to draw the pen across the paper as Worver sat back to pet his twisted little pet.

Before he could complete the first stroke, Jace and the others threw open the door.

"*Ahja. Za-fayn ha'alikk hamza Ebano Bakr Sayf al-Din ibn Ceham.*" The mesmerist's robes were torn and bloodied, frayed by acid and ragged at his wrists, but his regal bearing and intense purple eyes made these seem embellishments worthy of a king. "Greetings."

"Not again! He's a madman!" Mysos surged up out of the chair, readying his spells. Ebano did not flinch, his purple eyes flashing as if eager for the challenge—but he also did not draw his hands out or speak words in the magical tongue. Mysos paused in his casting, unwilling to start throwing spells around in such a small space, and Jace seized upon the opportunity to leap past Ebano toward Belen's side.

Belen and Worver rose up out of their chairs, equally surprised. "What . . . but you . . . Hautos!" Worver called, pressing his hands to either side of his head as if the steam of anger might blow his top hat right off.

"Hautos is busy, ringmaster." Jace smirked. It felt good to have all the advantages on his side this time! Cerisse held two throwing darts ready, two more tucked into her belt, and Ebano folded his arms in a picture of supreme unconcern.

"Jace?" the White Robe looked even more confused. "Jace Pettier, the tightrope walker?"

"At your service, wizard of Palanthas." The boy's eyes moved from the wizard to the ringmaster, and settled gently on Belen. "Are you all right?" he asked her.

"Jace, you shouldn't be here," she whispered.

"Because you made a deal with the ringmaster? I know. But you should know that he didn't just tell Hautos to heal Ebano. He also told him to kill Ebano—right after the contract was signed."

"I think you should stay and hear the story, ringmaster." Cerisse moved in closer, pressing the sharp end of her throwing dart an inch from Worver's throat. While Mysos was listening to the boy, Worver had been moving slowly toward the back door—only to find himself stopped point first by the half-elf's weapons.

"What is going on here?" Mysos demanded. "I won't have these proceedings interrupted with exaggerations. If Worver treats you poorly or doesn't pay you enough, then that is a separate issue. I will be happy to discuss it after the issues with Belen and Angvale are finished, but this is a matter of Solamnian law—"

"This *is* about Belen and Angvale," the boy insisted. Jace straightened, hurling a harsh stare at the ringmaster. "Belen attacked that village."

Mysos threw his hands into the air. "I already know that! The dragon has confessed—"

"To the attack yes, but she didn't kill anyone!" Jace clenched his fists.

Ebano stepped forward, the scrape of the mystic's patterned slippers on the wood floor keeping Mysos's attention divided. The mesmerist locked eyes with Mysos, returning the White Robe's angry stare with a somber peace. Whatever was going on, Ebano wanted Mysos to pay attention to this boy. Out of respect for the other wizard's power—or perhaps to get to the bottom of this—Mysos stopped protesting. "Tell me."

"The people who lived in Angvale are still alive. They've just been changed into werewolves, cursed by a powerful magic because they failed to protect a sacred stone. Belen didn't kill anyone! But there's more—the attack wasn't her fault. She was tricked into thinking that the village stole her egg—threatened her child—and she went there to get it back. She thought she was doing the right thing. Belen was thinking like a mother, not like a killer."

"Do you have any idea who would do such a thing?" Mysos asked.

"I do."

"How terrible that those poor people are still alive! And cursed too!" Worver interrupted swiftly. He tsk-tsked, waving his hands in the air. His pet, Tsusu, climbed up into the wagon's rafters, hissing softly. Worver snatched up the contract on the table and fluttered it at the wizard. "Master Mysos, let's finish what we were doing. Once the contract is signed, we'll have plenty of time to sit down and discuss this. As you know, Jace fell from quite a height the other day. I think he struck his head, you see—"

Mysos shushed the ringmaster with a sharp gesture of his hand. "Jace?"

"Worver did it all, sir. He lied to Belen about her egg—it was taken by the evil dragons—and he stole Angvale's magic stone. He enslaved the pukah who serve it, just like he's enslaving those werewolves he had performing today. The pukah have been doing work for the circus for five years, ever since he took the stone. Worver did all of this for his own benefit. He's known about this the whole time, even when he found Belen in the woods, and he's been keeping it secret. Even now, he wants you and Belen to sign that contract"—Jace pointed at it—"and make her a slave too."

"Do you have any proof?"

"He's got the stone in one of the circus wagons, sir." Jace insisted. "He's got some kind of key around his neck, something that makes him officially the owner of the stone."

Mysos turned to Worver, stepping past Belen and, perhaps foolishly, turning his back on the dark foreign mage. If this was some sort of a trick, he'd know it soon enough. "Well, Worver?"

"I have no idea what the boy's babbling about, master wizard." Worver straightened, ignoring the dart. "He's always blamed me, you know, for his father's fall. This is all a nasty trick to get even with me for what he sees as his family's failure! You know as well as I that Jace was going to fall from that rope before you arrived—you saved his life! But Jace is stubborn, and he's vengeful enough to make all this up just to get Belen's attention. Everyone knows he has a crush on her, and he'd do anything—including lie, cheat, and steal—to show off for her."

Jace's heart fell through his feet. He felt his face turn red as Belen blinked and looked at him, and even redder when Cerisse looked away. "That . . . that has nothing . . . to do with this!" he stammered. Belen looked surprised, but the worst thing of all was the pitying softness in her stare. Jace's vision blurred and he pushed past Ebano angrily. "Stop blaming me!"

"Ah, son, the truth hurts, doesn't it? It must be hard. You know she's a dragon? Belen is older and more mature than you will ever be, and she's far more powerful. You're nothing but a little circus tramp, barely a tenth her age! Of course she's not interested in you. Now end this charade, get out of my wagon, and we'll all let bygones be bygones." Worver preened while Tsusu's hissing laughter echoed faintly in the shadows.

"You shut up!" Cerisse snarled, pushing the tip of her dart against Worver's throat. "Jace is wonderful. He's smart, and he's brave, and even Belen would be lucky to have him!" Her outburst was unexpectedly fierce, her red hair lashing back and forth like a tiger's tail.

"Cerisse! You can't believe this ridiculous tale. Master Mysos, I assure you, this is all fantasy!"

"Very well, I'm willing to accept that." Mysos folded his arms.

"You are?" Worver brightened

"Of course. But just in case, why don't you show me what you're wearing around your neck?"

The ringmaster's face fell. "Surely that isn't necessary."

"I think it is. In fact, I insist."

Worver's hands fumbled as he slowly raised them to his neckline. "Master Mysos, of course I'll do anything you require. I only ask that you be gentle on the poor boy when you realize what a liar he's being. It isn't his fault, you know. His father's tragic fall, the pressure on Jace to redeem an entire family filled with failures and reprobates—"

"Hey!" Jace yelped, stung again.

"I'm trying to do what's best, my boy. Here we are, my necklace." Worver pulled it out of his neckline with a quick tug. "You'll see it's everything you expected—and more."

The thin cord around Worver's neck was unassuming, made of light leather looping down to a wooden trinket on the end. Jace had been anticipating something more grand—a holy symbol of Chislev, perhaps, or a magical token—but instead, it was only a child's whistle made of wood. Before anyone could react, Worver lifted it to his lips and blew.

Light instantly coalesced around him, blinding them all. Jace heard a scuffle. Tsusu's thin laugh darted down from the rafters, bounding to the floor and away. He heard Cerisse scream, and then came Ringmaster Worver's voice, smug in the white nothingness. "Obey me, my pukah minions."

As the brilliance faded, six bright lights became more distinct, swirling in patterns around Worver's heavy form.

"Kill the boy, the girl, and the hypnotist. Use your magic to make the dragon girl forget again. It seems your little spell fails under too close inspection. Oh, and erase the White Robe's memories too. Make sure he signs that contract." The fairies turned on Mysos and the others, unable to resist the command of the whistle's wielder.

Worver smiled, twisting his mustache as Tsusu leaped up on his shoulder. Jace could see that the monkeylike creature already had blood on its hands, and the girl on the floor wasn't moving. Worver stepped backward through the curtains at the front of the wagon where Cerisse had come in. "Oh, and clean up when you're finished, my little pets. We can't afford to have any loose ends."

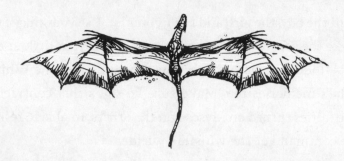

CHAPTER SIXTEEN

The pukah dived toward them with thin, shrill screeches, claws outstretched, and wings buzzing. The inside of the wagon reflected their brilliant light from brass fixtures to mirrors to glass. Anything and everything bright became illuminated like a hundred candles as the pukah rushed forward.

Jace yelled to the others, "Don't hurt them! They're slaves, it's not their fault!" He didn't know if Mysos would listen or if Ebano would understand, but Belen would know what to do. He looked for any way he could fight, picking up a bucket to swing at the pukah that launched itself into his hair. With a scream, Jace flinched away, swinging the bucket wildly in an attempt to trap the creature inside.

The pukah was far too quick for him, dodging under the lip of the bucket and renewing its attack. Its wings left silvery patterns in the air, scattering dust across Jace's shoulders and face. He tried not to breathe in, but was unable to avoid it, and a strange lightness tickled through his lungs.

"Don't breathe their dust!" Belen was yelling. It seemed tinny and far away. "It's magic!"

Magic? Like Belen's dancing. Pretty. Shiny too. Jace looked down at the bucket in his hands and tried to remember what he'd been doing. Feeding some animal? Getting water? That seemed like a strange thing to be doing inside one of the wagons. Was he about to go on stage? Tightrope walking with a bucket. The idea made him giggle. He should go find Cerisse and tell her about it. Maybe she'd juggle buckets in her next act too.

A stiff wind nearly knocked Jace over, slamming him back against the wall of the wagon. The bucket tumbled from his hands, forgotten, and sparkling dust swirled past him, cleared away by the wind. Jace looked up and saw Mysos standing with one hand outstretched, wind whipping his pale robes about him. "Thanks," Jace managed, and the mage nodded once. "Where's Worver?"

"Outside." Belen was kneeling by a fallen figure on the floor. "Cerisse—she's badly hurt."

The same cold, horrible feeling Jace felt when he was falling swept over him now.

"Duck, Jace!" Mysos yelled before the young man could

ask more, and Jace instinctively did as he'd been told.

A pukah swooshed past his head, carrying one of Worver's cooking knives. That would have taken off an ear at least! Jace yelped and reached for his sword, but Ebano knocked his hand aside.

"No room." Ebano glared. "One must use the right tool for the right job."

Another giggle bubbled up uncomfortably in Jace's throat. Ebano almost made sense that time. Stumped, Jace looked around for the bucket again as another pukah carrying a pair of sharp spurs swept toward Belen. She screamed, throwing up her arm, and the pukah swooshed past, leaving three long bloody scrapes from shoulder to elbow. Two more were fighting Mysos, scattering their dust all about the White Robe, trying to catch him in their spell. Mysos continued controlling the wind, trying to avoid the sparkling residue and also keep the pukah off-balance in the air. "If they take his memory"—Jace pointed—"we're all done for! Ebano, don't you have any spells left?"

The hypnotist shook his head. He spun and began tearing apart the ringmaster's bed, tearing away the sheets and blankets. Mystified, Jace turned back to the fight, swinging his bucket through the air and doing his best to hold his breath. Worver was getting away, he realized.

"All my offensive spells would either burn the wagon down or kill the pukah," Mysos called out. "We have to find a way to capture them."

"Yeah, we're working on it!" Jace scowled, swinging the bucket wide.

One of the pukah thunked into the bucket, but before Jace could slam something over it, the fairy kicked against the side of the metal with enough strength to rip the handle out of Jace's hand. It fell to the floor, bucket, pukah, and all. Jace leaped atop it, holding the bucket down with all of his weight as the pukah kicked and slammed into the little metal container. Dust puffed out from beneath it anytime the bucket tipped up—which was a lot. "Got one!"

Belen, who was huddled over Cerisse on the ground, was bleeding from a number of scratches. Mysos stood over her, using his wind powers to keep the dust away, but he could do little against the physical attacks of the pukah, who tore at him and Belen with ever-increasing desperation. They hurled knives, flew close with blunt weapons to strike and bash, and trilled dust into the air with their sparkling wings. Sooner or later, there would be so much dust in the air that Mysos's spell wouldn't be much use.

"Jace!" Ebano called. "Let go. Take this!" He gestured wildly, flapping a big, thick quilt in the air. Trusting the dark-skinned man, Jace let go of the bucket, releasing a very disoriented and very angry pukah. Jace lunged for one end of the blanket, grateful that he had good balance as he was forced to dodge through the mess of slippery dust and rolling goods all over the wagon floor. He grabbed ahold, and Ebano grinned. "Sweep!"

Sweep? That was his big plan?

Then with a flash, Jace understood. Ebano began swooshing the blanket through the air, twisting it back and forth with Jace as the central point. The wide flaps caught around the pukah, and Ebano would twist again, catching the little creatures up in the folds of cloth. It was like a strange dance with Ebano bounding through the wagon, sweeping up the pukah and twirling the blanket about. Jace tried to follow him, helping to hold the folds shut when Ebano caught one, laughing out loud at the strangeness of it all. Mysos began to shift his wind control, blowing the pukah into the blanket with each swoop of his arms. When the blanket was full, Ebano took the other end from Jace, wrapping up the pukah inside and tying the ends of the blanket into a firm knot.

"Jace!" Belen cried. "We've got to get Cerisse help."

Leaving Mysos and Ebano to catch the rest of the pukah, Jace knelt beside Belen on the floor. Cerisse was unconscious, her auburn hair dark with blood. There was a wound on her chest, near her shoulder, and despite the fact that Belen had twisted cloth against it and bound it as best she could, Cerisse's face was far too pale, and her breathing was slight.

"It's all right." The words tumbled out of Jace's mouth in an uneven rush. "We'll get her to the stone. We'll have the pukah heal her. They healed Ebano, she'll be fine. They can't hurt Cerisse. She's got to stay."

"Jace." Belen caught his arm before he could scoop up Cerisse to carry her. "The pukah can't help her. The stone can't do anything unless its owner commands it, and Worver has the whistle." She didn't say what she was obviously thinking—that every moment they sat here, Worver got farther and farther away.

Worver. Jace surged to his feet. "We have to stop him. Ebano, Mysos, can you handle the pukah?"

"Go, Jace," Mysos answered. "We'll tie them up and do what we can for Cerisse."

Ebano agreed, nodding to the girl on the floor. Jace grabbed his arm, regardless of the writhing quilt Ebano was clutching. "I'm coming back, Ebano. All right? Do you understand? I'll return. Don't let anything happen to Cerisse. Don't let her die."

Ebano's eyes sparked, and he seemed taken aback. "Return," he repeated. Then, a slow nod. "This one understands."

"Good." Belen said. She was already halfway through the curtains when Jace caught her elbow. "Belen, are you sure you want to do this? If Worver finds a way to catch you or get that forgetting dust on you again—"

"If I don't go, I can't avenge the people of Angvale. And anyway"—she managed a faint smile—"I can fly, and you won't catch him on foot."

"Fine." He smiled, keeping his hand on her arm. "We'll go together."

They ran to the clearing outside the big top, the only place on the circus grounds where there was enough room for a dragon. They were only a few feet from the opening to the main event, and Jace could hear the crowd inside, roaring over some fantastic trick. Belen focused herself, slipping between forms with a graceful gesture. Her body glowed and shimmered, the silver of her hair smoothing over her skin as her luminous gray eyes caught the light. She grew smoothly, too fast for the eye to follow, wings lifting from her sides to catch the wind. In only a moment, she was a dragon again, regal and resplendent, the sun shimmering from her scales as if they were the fine armor of a Knight of Solamnia. Jace couldn't help but take a moment to look at her. She was so beautiful, so graceful and real—but even as he did, he felt his heart give a little twinge. Cerisse was in danger.

Belen lowered her forearm, allowing Jace to climb up onto her leg and pull himself to her back. He buried his hands in her silvery frill once more, wrapping his legs tight about her shoulders as the dragon shifted its weight for a lunge. They launched into the air with a single push of Belen's back legs, her massive wings pounding the air as she gained altitude. In the wake of her takeoff, the big top fluttered and tore, canvas ripping wide along the seams under the thrust of the wind swept by dragon's wings. Jace could hear yells inside, followed by screams and oohs as the main canvas fell away. A thousand faces stared up at them, ignoring the circus act to watch the glittering silver body of the dragon swoop into the sky.

"Worver's Amazing Celestial Circus of Light," Jace muttered to himself with a smile. "Now with real dragons."

"I see his wagon!" Belen called back after only a few moments of flight. "He's got the stone too! Poor Hautos. Looks like Worver dumped him and everything else out onto the ground so the wagon would go faster. Worver's all alone in there!"

"That's good news, right?" Jace had to scream the words. Belen had never gone this fast before. The wind stung him, making his eyes tear up and reddening the skin on his cheeks and hands. He held on for dear life, ducking behind her long neck to keep out of the worst of it, feeling her wings sweep back and forth with more power than he'd imagined.

"No! The wagon's going very fast. He's headed for the woods. You remember how thick they are?"

"You couldn't land in them?"

"More than that! I can't fly beneath them either, and we won't be able to see the wagon from above the trees. We have to catch him before he gets to the trees! Climb down onto my leg again so you're closer!"

Jace did so, hand over hand as if he were going down the ladder from his tightrope. He tried to think of it the same way, just another step after step, safely clinging to the stability of Belen's leg. "And then what? He's not just going to stop when we get to him."

Belen was silent for a moment, the sound of her beating wings filling Jace's ears. "Then you'll just have to jump."

Jace froze, his fingers tightening around Belen's leg. Jump? Was she serious? They were forty feet up, and they'd have to stay high or Belen would crash into the trees. That was a farther fall than he had from the tightrope during his quadruple tuck with no net! Jace thought of his father, remembering the long moment before he struck the ground, the sickening crunch of bone. "I'll never make it!" he screamed, but the wind tore away his words and he wasn't sure the dragon heard him.

Jump. He'd launched himself from the dragon's wing to the chimera, but that was different. That was like being on a high wire, trusting your footing, being ready for the next step. It wasn't the same as hurling yourself straight at the ground—or worse, at a moving wagon. What if he missed? What if he didn't miss? Neither was a good result.

They pulled up behind the wagon, swooping closer with each rush of Belen's mighty wings. Jace tensed, trying to measure the distance. He might live. He might not even break too many bones. But still, the idea of jumping . . . just . . . *falling* . . .

"It's time, Jace!" Belen tried to stabilize her flight as low as she dared, the tree line of the woods rushing closer with every passing second. He could see Worver at the front of the wagon, looking up over his shoulder in terror as the dragon swooped low. Tsusu clung to the top canvas, shrieking in excitement, lashing its odd grayish tail eagerly as the wagon rocked and bounced toward the woods. Jace gulped. "Jace! Don't be afraid to fall!"

"Belen, I can't—"

"Just do it!"

He had to trust her. It was the only way—the only way to catch Worver, free Angvale, get the stone back, and help the circus and his friends. The only way to heal Cerisse.

Clenching his muscles and gathering his courage, Jace

let his fingers slide from Belen's scales. He leaped toward the wagon, keeping it firmly fixed in his mind as the place—the only place—he was going to land. Right there. On the canvas. Right on top of that squirming little beast, Tsusu, if he could help it.

Free-falling through the air, Jace had all the time in the world to watch the world go past. He thought he'd be afraid as he felt everything spin out of balance around him, but it wasn't like that at all. Jace spread his body as wide as he could to slow the speed of his decline. He'd fallen before, from high wires and trapezes, but never like this—this was almost like flying. When he fell from the wire, it was a mistake, a flaw in his technique or a problem with his balance. He hadn't messed up here. He wasn't wrong, or broken, or less than the other performers for falling. He'd *chosen* this to save his friends. No matter what happened, the feeling was liberating.

Never look at the ground, his father had taught him. *Not even when you're falling. It never helps.*

Jace gulped. Was it bad luck to be thinking of his dad at a time like this?

The wagon rushed up at him with amazing speed, the trees of the forest smacking his legs and arms as he fell. He hadn't realized how close they'd been to the forest—how nearly he'd come to missing their only opportunity.

When Jace slammed into the wagon, he closed his eyes and thought of Cerisse. She'd be so mad if he didn't make it home.

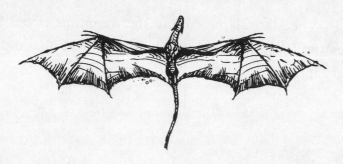

CHAPTER SEVENTEEN

The wagon lurched from Jace's impact. The axles broke and the canvas around the top of the arched storage area shrieked and collapsed. The horses screamed, redoubling their speed despite the fact that two of the wheels were now lopsided, causing the wagon to careen wildly from one side of the road to the other. Worver barely hung on, clinging to the reins with one hand while he drew his short whip with the other.

Jace burst up from the wreckage in the rear, sword in his hand, feeling more alive than he had in years. He shouted—not a cry of fear or rage, but a sheer exultation of joy. With a whoop he jumped out of the shreds of canvas and the broken boards and used his short sword to block Worver's first attack, smashing through the ringmaster's hastily raised forearm to land a punch right on Worver's thick chin.

The ringmaster staggered and dropped the reins. The

horses ran wild, racing through the woods and dragging the broken wagon behind them, panicked by the dragon in the air. No longer shackled by leather reins, Worver was able to make his second attack come faster, and his whip scored a long red welt across Jace's cheek and neck, ripping open the shoulder of his tunic as it hit.

From behind, there was a high-pitched shriek. Scrabbling claws sank into Jace's back, tearing into his flesh as if they were a handful of needles stabbing at his skin. Jace reached back over his shoulder, trying to grasp Tsusu, but the creature scrambled back and forth, evading Jace's grip. "My quasit has you now, boy!" Worver snarled, raising the whip again. "You're just like your father, always poking into things. If he hadn't been so interested in the new dancer and her background, I might not have had Tsusu loosen his tightrope!"

Shocked and enraged, Jace felt as if he had all the power of a dragon. He slammed himself backward against the ruins of the wagon top, crushing Tsusu against the wood. The wretched creature cried out and fell. Jace used the opportunity to kick Worver directly in the stomach. The ringmaster toppled, falling to the side of the wagon. He gripped the railing in order to stay on. The wagon wheels spun only inches from the man's face, flicking mud all over his splendid red jacket.

Jace spun, thrusting his sword down toward the creature. Tsusu wriggled to the side and the blade missed him. The creature spat a thick, poisonous goo up toward Jace's face. The boy ducked aside just in time, and the spittle landed on the wooden wreckage, hissing and eating through the wood in seconds. Jace twisted, stabbing down again—and this time his sword caught the quasit squarely. The creature let out a burbling wail as it clutched the sword blade, and then began to laugh. As Jace watched, the creature melted away, turning to goo and slime right on his sword. The metal blade hissed and melted along with Tsusu, obliterated by the horrible gunk. Jace dropped the ruined hilt, staring at the smoking, hissing spot where the quasit had once been.

"Tsusu!" Worver was pulling himself up onto the wagon once more, grabbing his whip back for another strike. He spun on Jace in a fury. "You wretched little boy!"

Jace ducked and felt the burn of Worver's whip as it lashed along his injured back. The stroke burned like fire, opening welts between his shoulder blades. Trees flashed past on both sides as the woods enveloped the two, casting shadows across the wagon. Occasional bursts of sunlight shone through the trees, blinding Jace in patches. Worver reached back again to bring the whip about, and Jace stepped in to grapple him.

The ringmaster was much larger than Jace and more used to fighting in tight quarters—likely due to his background taming circus animals—but Jace had the advantage of steady footing. He was used to shifting surfaces, so the loping, teetering wagon was no problem at all. Worver tugged, trying to hurl the boy off the wagon, but Jace balanced himself against the ringmaster's weight, twisting around so that Worver was on the outside. Worver continued the motion unexpectedly, lurching forward and toppling Jace to the wooden floor of the driver's seat.

"I'll kill you," Worver hissed, struggling to get his hands around the boy's neck. "I'll kill you, just like I killed that red-haired juggler girl!"

Rage surged through Jace, giving him the strength to shove Worver off. He rolled, gripped the reins that dangled on the wagon seat, and pulled with all of his might. The horses screamed in protest, turning in their tracks, dragging the broken wagon to the side. Worver stood over Jace, raising his whip once more and aiming at the boy's throat.

The wagon careened into a tree. There was a horrible impact, and Jace was thrown from the wagon as if he were a feed bag, turning end over end until he landed amid brush and pine needles. Jace knew how to fall, so he rolled with it, feeling every sharp spike of thorn and needle against his injured back. He raised his head from the ground and saw the horses run off into the forest, dragging their traces behind them. The wagon remained, a broken pile of wood wrapped halfway around a majestic oak.

Jace dragged himself to his feet and picked up a broken board that had been flung from the wreckage. He marched toward the wagon, every step full of pain. There, near the tree, Worver was climbing to his feet, still holding the whip in his hand. His red coat was torn to shreds, his tie twisted to one side and his top hat lost amid the wreckage. Fixing his blinking eyes on Jace, Worver shakily raised the whip to hit him again.

Jace hit him squarely in the face with the board, planting him flat on his back. He lifted the cord from the unconscious Worver's neck, taking away the little wooden whistle that controlled the stone of Angvale. "The people of Angvale are about to become your greatest audience of all, ringmaster. For your final trick, you're going to give them back everything you took away." Jace held up the whistle, imagining the smile Cerisse would give him when he told her he'd saved the day.

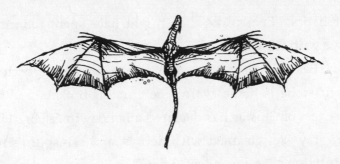

CHAPTER EIGHTEEN

The sound of drums and flute music echoed through the dell, and the trees seemed alight with happiness and sunlight. Amid the dell, the restoration of the houses and buildings of Angvale had paused for a day of celebration and amusement. The circus had come to town.

In the center of the white-cobblestone square, the stone of Chislev—festooned with ribbons and flowers—rose from a flower bed, marking the center of the village. Children chased one another, carrying brightly colored pinwheels made of paper, shouting about the acrobats that were building a human pyramid near the center of the square. White sparkling lights darted here and there, dodging from branch to branch in a whirling, frenetic dance to the sounds of laughter.

"I see the pukah are getting along well." Jace smiled at the sight of them, his eyes following their whirling acrobatics. "Looks like they might have spent too much time with the circus."

Belen laughed. "Can you blame them for being excited? Their stone is home again, the curse is broken, and the priestess of Chislev has declared a holiday in celebration." Her gray eyes gleamed with delight and she spun, silver hair flying. "It's a wonderful day!"

"Lady Belen." The white-robed mage had caught sight of them and was crossing the cobbled street through the press of crowds to greet them. "I see you're in fine spirits."

"Wizard Mysos!" Belen curtsied. "Thank you. You've done so much for Angvale!"

"Thank me? For what? Nearly putting you in jail? Missing the mark so completely that I nearly bound you to an evil man's service?" Mysos shook his head. The wrinkles around his eyes were deeper than they had been only a few weeks ago, his countenance even more stonelike and sober. "No, lady. I may have been a catalyst, but I am not the one who helped you discover the truth." Mysos bowed to Jace, inclining his head in respect. "Without this boy and his friends, I fear this happy village might be a very different place."

Pride swelled Jace's chest. "I'm glad to have helped."

"Have you seen that fellow Ebano about?" Mysos craned his head to see over a rank of fire-breathers lighting up the air with their craft. "I've managed to pick up a few words of his language and was rather hoping to say farewell before I head back to Palanthas."

"I'm sure he's here somewhere. He wouldn't miss the big day!" Jace took in the bright colors and flash of the festival, reveling in the joy of the villagers. Mysos took his leave of them, catching someone else in the crowd whom he wanted to greet, and Belen and Jace headed for the central square. They walked onward through the press of people to watch as the fire-breathers finished their act to raucous applause. Quickly clearing away their equipment, they fled the square with waves and cheers to let the next group come in. These were the jugglers, dancing with painted belaying pins, brightly colored balls, or gleaming silver hoops in their hand.

"Jace, look!" Belen pointed ahead through the crowd. An old woman was lifting children onto a pony, her brown and green robes beautifully embroidered despite the simple homespun from which they were made. Her hair was still wild and twiglike, but now it looked more like branches in springtime than a barren or twisted tree. The wooden whistle hung on a simple leather cord around her neck. "The priestess of Chislev!"

"She's still scary." Jace shivered. "Even without a pack of werewolves following her around."

Belen's laugh was as bright as the sunlight through the trees. "You were more afraid of her than you were of Worver."

"Yeah, well, Worver was a known evil. I'm glad that the White Robes of Palanthas have taken him away. He'll make a really great street sweeper."

"If Worver scrubs Palanthas's streets for seventy-three years, do you think he can get them all clean?"

"I'll stop by and stomp mud on them every day just to keep him busy." Jace scowled playfully.

"I don't think you're going anywhere near Palanthas," Belen said. "Not with your new responsibilities."

"What do you mean?"

"Well, I'm told there's a very good up-and-comer ready to try the quadruple tuck flip."

Jace raised his eyebrows.

"This is why I had a rope strung between the schoolhouse and the general store, so he can show me what he's made of."

"You're kidding!"

She took his hand and pulled him toward the schoolhouse with a gentle smile. Indeed, there above the little garden plaza hung a taut thread of thick acrobatic rope, secured professionally at both ends. Jace stared at it, half thrilled, half terrified. "Jace," Belen pulled him to a stop a little distance from the ladder. "You need to stop being afraid."

"I won't be afraid if you're here."

She shook her head. "I can't go with the circus. I have to stay here in Angvale and help repair the damage I caused. These people are rebuilding their houses and their lives—and I need to help make that happen."

Jace turned to her, a lump in his throat. "But . . . Belen. I need you."

"No, Jace. You don't."

"But I lov— "

"Jace." Her stern expression stopped him midword. "Stop. You don't love me. You love the idea of me. I'm a dragon, not a woman. I'm much older than you, and our lives are very different."

"I don't care, Belen!" he protested. "I'll stay here with you. I'm sure I could be useful to Angvale."

"You'd give up everything that you are, ruin your life, and stay here?" Her words were painful, but her expression was caring. "That would be wrong for you, Jace, and wrong for me to expect it. But more than that . . . the truth is, Jace, I care about you very much, but I don't love you. Not in the way you want me to. But I don't think you love me that way either."

"I know what I feel."

"You know you care for me, Jace, but you and I are so different that it's easy for you to dream about me without risking anything. You know that it can never happen, so you don't have to try and risk failing. That's not what love is, Jace. Love is all about risk. It's all about reaching out to someone, and finding—miraculously—that they share your dreams and hopes, and that you share theirs. I want you to find someone who can give you as much as you give them. That's not me, Jace."

He sighed. What Belen said made sense, and more, he could feel in his heart that she was right. He cared for Belen, and he could see himself with her—but how? As someone like the chimera might have been, doing nothing more important than cleaning Belen's tower while she was doing important dragon things? "You're right, as always. I hate that."

They laughed together, and Jace felt a weight lift off of his shoulders.

"Don't worry. I'm going to visit the circus when the village is rebuilt," Belen said. I might even do a few command performances from time to time." She smiled, hugging him. "Now hurry up. I want to see that high wire act. And Jace? Don't be afraid to fall."

"I know!" he yelled back, jogging to the ladder and swinging up it. "Mysos is in the audience!"

"That wasn't what I . . . " She said more, but he couldn't hear her over the roar of the crowd. The villagers had seen him climbing to the tightrope, and they clapped and whistled and yelled their approval while he rose higher and higher.

The tightrope stretched out before him, a glistening silk thread forty feet above the upturned faces and waving hands. Jace stepped out onto it, feeling it shift beneath his careful balance. Each step was a cautious one, testing the rope's weight and tension, edging out over the crowd. This was where he felt most at home, with the wind in his hair and the solitary feeling of hovering above the world. Was this how Belen felt when she flew alone in the clouds? As if she'd found somewhere that she really belonged? If so, then this was as close to being a dragon as Jace was ever going to get, and he loved it.

He began to shift his weight, causing the rope to bounce up and down, hefting him farther upward with each thrumming motion. Jace looked down at the crowd, waving to them in anticipation of his final jump—and there, standing among his friends and well-wishers, her auburn hair loose and flowing to her waist, was Cerisse.

Don't be afraid to fall. Belen's words echoed in his ears as he smiled down at his half-elf friend. Find someone who shares your dreams, and live them fully.

Jace smiled, and his feet left the tightrope. He tucked himself tightly, rotating in the air like one of the dancing pukah fairies, feeling the earth and sky switch places again . . . and again . . . and again . . . and then, after his fourth rotation, he snapped his legs back down, finding the tightrope beneath him, waiting to catch him before he fell. He straightened, spreading his arm, as the music below swelled.

Jace grinned and waved both arms toward the roaring, exalting crowd, but Cerisse's glowing face stood out among them, trusting, believing in him completely. *Don't be afraid to fall*, he repeated to himself, finally understanding what Belen had been trying to tell him.

"I won't, Belen. Thanks to you."

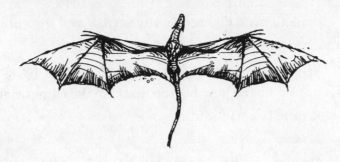

Epilogue

Slippered footsteps trampled the dust of the road, pressing the ground with eager motion. He did not say goodbye to them—how could he have expressed so full a heart knowing so few words? As he walked, he prayed for their futures to be happy and bright. His journey to Khur would be a long one and the trials many, but none more meaningful than the battle already won within the traveler's spirit, the one that had renewed his heart. Hope, long dead and buried, had been rekindled. A belief that good dragons still existed within the world was restored. He had thought them all dead and gone, that all dragons were like the terrible Green who had destroyed his people.

If a good dragon could be found who would give her life to protect innocents, if a mere circus performer could defeat an evil curse, and a wizard of death could fight for the side of light, then perhaps, just perhaps, she could be alive after all.

Amani, my daughter. In my sorrow and my guilt, I abandoned you.

With one word, the brave boy who fought for good dragons told Ebano how he, too, could make things right.

Return, Jace had said.

Return.

My name is Ebano Bakr Sayf al-Din ibn Ceham, prince of Sayf, of the grand tribe of Khur. I have traveled many lands and seen many wonders, praise Keja who united us and curse his seven sons. The truth has been revealed to me, my family taken from me, and I bear the hope of silver dragons and the dream of redemption in my heart. Hear my prayer, noble gods—let me find her and set us both free.

Alak-al-saham-din-al-bhar, may the blessings of the gods be upon the world.

About the Author

R.D. Henham is a scribe in the great library of Palanthas. In the course of transcribing stories of legendary dragons, the author felt a gap existed in the story of the everydragon: ordinary dragons who end up doing extraordinary things. With the help of fellow scribes, R.D. has filled that gap with this series of books based on Sindri Suncatcher's remarkable *A Practical Guide to Dragons*.

About the Author's Assistant

Ree Soesbee has assisted R.D. Henham with several books in the Dragon Codex series, including *Black Dragon Codex*. She is the author of seven books in the Dragonlance: The New Adventures series, as well as several other books for children and young adults. She lives in Seattle with the Grand Adventuress of Cats and a healthy perspective of her place in the world. She studies aikido and Socrates, which leads to interesting internal conversations. You can find her website at www.learsfool.com.

Unlock the secret of the gold dragon!

The blue dragon, Lazuli, lives to torment the villagers of Anders's hometown, Hartfall. He demands more and more, until the baron, Anders's father, has only one thing to give: himself. Lazuli will arrive at midnight to take the baron away. Anders has one hope left: the gold dragon that sits silently watching atop a ledge above the village. In one legendary battle Lazuli magically petrified the gold dragon, once Hartfall's sworn protector. But Anders is sure he can find a way to awaken the beast. In the dead of night, he sneaks out onto the gold dragon's ledge, and there he stumbles onto a secret that throws everything he thought he knew about his home and his family into question. Can Anders unlock the secret of the gold dragon in time to save his village—and his dad?

GOLD
DRAGON CODEX

Available January 2010